JEFFREY W. AUBUCHON

Three Desert Stories

92252 PRESS

For desert friends,
especially Bouhouch.

The Moon watches in wonder as her brother's chariot scorches clouds and thunderheads, and the earth bursts into flame, the crests of the mountains first, and then, as the moisture of rocks comes to a sudden boil, in loud, random explosions. Trees are consumed, and grain in an instant ripens to ash.

Earth, having nowhere to hide, felt how her streams were dying and turned her scorched face to the skies in pain to complain, raising her hand to shield her eyes so mountains trembled.

—Ovid, *The Metamorphoses*, Book II
Lines 206-210 & 268-270

Contents

Foreword

Sahara as Symbol in Later Twentieth-Century North African Literature

Indigenous North African and Euro-American writers use the Sahara as a symbol for greater meaning in twentieth-century literature. Some writers, like Ibrahim al-Koni (Libyan) and Miral al-Tahawy (Egyptian), present the desert as a wasteland—at first glance empty and then surprisingly full of activity. These authors describe a desolate place, but also a cauldron of magical realism that often draws on mythological antecedents. European and American writers like Paul Bowles portray the Sahara and its people with an outsider's eye, describing a setting that often acts as a character itself and serves as a space for wandering. Nobel Laureates Naguib Mahfous (Egyptian) and J.M.G. Leclézio (French), as well as Mohammed Dib (Algerian) and Alifa Rifaat (Egyptian), are other authors with whom I situate my stories.

Both "wasteland" and "wander" are important words for my writing. I take "wasteland" from the local descriptions of the area surrounding the great Bou Gafr—a fearsome mountain where the Ait 'Atta tribesmen of southern Morocco unsuccessfully resisted the French project of "pacification" in 1933. I prefer "wander" over travel because of its resonance with wonder, but it also suggests a sense of purposelessness in reading these texts and in crafting my own. Wander—like the Scottish verb *stravaig*—indicates activity, but also seems more reflective, and less definite, than the act of traveling. The wanderer perceives as extraordinary that which might be commonplace to the traveler. For all of these authors, and myself, the desert is not just geography but a sanctuary for the spirit. This collection of three short stories: "Dylan," "Bou Gafr," and "Maryam," similarly present the Sahara both as a wasteland of magical realism and a place to wander.

Writing about North Africa from an American perspective, as in this project, poses some significant cultural challenges. In his 1979 book *Orientalism*, Edward Said argues that the discourse surrounding Western representations of the East (including the Middle East and, by extension, North Africa) has resulted in the coercion of the East by the West. "Orientalism," Said wrote, "is fundamentally a political doctrine willed over the Orient because the Orient was weaker than the West, which elided the Orient's difference with its weakness" (204). For Said, the Western cultural tradition has been presented as one of domination and a serious threat to those around the world who cannot escape such a culture by means of trade, travel, literature, or education. Through the Orientalist discourse, the East emerges as unchanging, whereas the story of the West reflects dynamic growth and change of the contemporary period.

Even Bowles, with his demonstrated admiration for North African life, could not write without a limited degree of Orientalism. I have similar concerns in my own work. A desire to hear authentic North African voices has influenced the authors I read and that shaped my original fiction. Claude Lévi-Strauss aptly demonstrates the tension between realism and caricature in his *Triste Tropiques* by writing, "either I can be like some traveler of the olden days, who was faced with a stupendous spectacle, all, or almost all, of which eluded him, or worse still, filled him with scorn and disgust; or I can be a modern traveler, chasing after the vestiges of a vanished reality" (43). I also aim to chase after those "vestiges of a vanished reality," to capture the essential while mindful of the Orientalist problem—particularly in character development—in my own fiction.

These stories follow the misadventures of a young American Peace Corps volunteer assigned to a remote Moroccan outpost on the Sahara's edge. I assign equal importance to the descriptions of place as well as the hero's growth. While the three short stories stand independently, they also work collectively using the desert as a symbol for wasteland, a place of wander, and a canvas for magical realism. Significant spans of time—first a stretch of seventeen months and then six more—punctuate the works as the protagonist grows.

I first encountered desert symbolism as a high school student with Willa Cather's 1927 novel, *Death Comes for the Archbishop*. The book remained important to me through college and my first journey to North Africa some ten years later. Cather's sparse prose attracted me from the beginning. As the story opens, her hero priest becomes lost in the arid wilderness of nineteenth-century New Mexico. Cather describes not only the landscape, but the tension between its features and featureless-ness: "The difficulty was that the country in which he found himself was so featureless—or, rather, that it was crowded with features, all exactly alike. As far as he could see, on every side, the landscape was heaped up into monotonous red sand-hills, not much larger than haycocks, and very much the shape of haycocks." Cather's words made me, as a teenage reader, yearn to see something other than the green hills of New England. I first encountered the desert in California's Mojave, but then it was off to North Africa before, in my later thirties, I finally arrived in Santa Fe.

Cather then places her main character, the French Bishop Latour, in this American wilderness: "He had been riding among them since early morning, and the look of the country had no more changed than if he had stood still." Movement—perhaps even wander—was important for Cather as she continued, "He must have traveled through thirty miles of these conical red hills, winding his way in the narrow cracks between them, and he had begun to think that he would never see anything else" (17). In just five epigrammatic sentences, with few adjectives, Cather creates a vast and "monotonous" place filled with conical hills and, later, a wilderness "naked of vegetation except for small juniper trees" (17). When I arrived in Morocco a decade after first reading Cather, I assumed the North African terrain would be different from her New Mexico, and yet, I found it to be similarly vast, monotonous, and especially naked. In the same way, I try to describe in my fiction the mountains of southern Morocco to unfamiliar readers. Turning from Cather's American southwest to the Sahara of al-Koni, al-Tahawy, and Bowles, I have found descriptions that not only capture the desert as wasteland but also a place befitting both human triumph and tragedy as well as a space for the mystical.

Dylan

Dylan re-read what he had underlined on the folded paper as he lay in the single hotel bed. Seeing the common Arabic word made him laugh. *Insha'Allah! Ha! As if it was up to God that I get there.* With the paper, he kept a photograph of his sister and Kayla, which he glanced at before putting both on the cement floor and reached for his cheap Nokia phone. The dark, spartan room lacked a nightstand and the small yellow-tinted window did not let in much morning light from the alleyway. *I always liked Aly's smile in that picture. That was a good day, just the three of us. I think Aly would be proud of me today.* He switched off the cellphone alarm minutes before it was to ring at six—he liked being just ahead of schedule. Dylan passed the night restlessly, both because the prospect for the day ahead excited him, and also the discomfort of the lodging. He had, however, paid only $3 for the room with its unclean linen. *Let's go*, he encouraged himself aloud while putting the phone on the floor. *You've got to do this. The great adventure starts now.*

Four, he reminded himself as he slipped into his boxer shorts with pink and blue stripes, *Lily said to get to Boumalne by four this afternoon or I'll miss the ride to the village.*

1

He had met Lily, the Peace Corps volunteer he would replace, the night before in Marrakech. Dylan had traveled south from Fez where his training ended while Lily traveled north from her post in Ikniouen. Although they had met once during Dylan's training, this last forty-minute encounter over coffee served as their unofficial transfer of responsibility before Lily headed onwards to depart from Rabat. She had told him how to get to Ikniouen, and he methodically wrote the directions on the lined paper before folding it.

"I told Faiz and Bouhouch to look for you tomorrow afternoon. They're like the village godfathers. Faiz leaves Boumalne in his van at four. Don't miss the ride or you'll have to wait overnight in Boumalne. Trust me, you don't want to get stuck there. Got any questions?" she had asked.

"Nope. It'll be great. Can't wait to see it," he said boldly.

"The mountains are beautiful, for sure, but it gets lonely out there. Make village friends quickly; you'll need them more than they need you."

"I got this, don't worry," he had tried to reassure her. Lily's round face grinned.

"I'm sure you do. We all think we do. Just don't hesitate to email if you think of any other questions. Be sure to get to Boumalne by four on Thursday. Got it?"

He replayed the memory in his mind as he stretched in the hotel room. *How hard can this be? She didn't seem particularly rugged, and not nearly as tough as Kayla.* Even after two years in Morocco, Lily still looked American; she was curvy and her ponytail hung from a maroon UMass ball cap. Her ears were pierced, but she wore no earrings. *Sensible*, he thought. *It drove me nuts in training when the girls would wear makeup. Why bother?* Lily wore an expensive shirt from an American mountaineering shop. *I can't imagine that shirt got much active use here. If Lily can survive here in Morocco, this will be easy.*

Dylan had stashed most of his belongings in his massive backpack the night before. He put on new hiking pants over his boxer shorts and donned a green t-shirt that read Siena College—a gift from his cousin, Christine. He touched the painted letters on the shirt, thinking of her and their summers together as kids. *The beach. Aly was so little then, now she's almost graduated high school. Christine was so sweet to send the shirt as a going-away present.* Some of his friends gave him t-shirts from their respective colleges as parting gifts and these practical mementos appealed to Dylan's sentimental side. He pulled the shirt over his head and then put his faded grey and purple Williams "Ephs" ball cap over his tousled brown hair without bothering to comb it—*no need to look pretty here.* He stuffed the folded paper, photograph, and phone into his pocket. Lacing his boots, he stepped into the silent atrium to use the toilet at the end of the hall. The toilet was truly a water closet, squeezed into the space under the staircase by the builder. A dim light bulb protruded from the wall and a porcelain-lined hole sunk into the floor for Dylan to use. Bending his head to the slope of the ceiling, he did not try to aim for the hole since clearly no one else had in that cramped space. *This is nasty. Kayla would hate this.*

He washed his hands with a trickle of cold water in the hallway sink. Finding neither soap nor towel, he dried his hands on his pants as he returned to his room and found his small bottle of hand-sanitizer. *Better than nothing*, he supposed, and after vigorously rubbing his hands together with the gel, he lifted the monstrous pack onto his shoulders—and with it, all he had brought for two years. He strapped his small leather knapsack—his companion for many hikes—to the front of the backpack. The leather, now soft from years of use, reminded him of places he had seen. *Places with Kayla.* He took one more careful look around the small room to ensure he had collected everything. The room had served its purpose for the night. *Not gonna miss this place.*

The phone read 6:24. *Six minutes early. Mumtaz*, he praised himself with some Arabic.

Dylan felt his way down the dark staircase, having to descend two flights to reach the windowless lobby. He had planned his departure the night before and paid ahead so that he could leave early. The closed front door looked heavy with its ornamental wood. Reaching for the iron handle, he pulled hard, but it would not budge. *Shit. I didn't think to ask when they unlock the door.* He pulled again. *Useless.* The dark reception had no bell to ring. He looked at his phone—6:28—and remembered 4:00. Alone, anxious, and very much in the dark, he felt his face become warm. *How am I going to get there in time?*

"*Pardon, pardon!*" The voice coming from the shadowy corner startled Dylan and he quickly turned around. The figure, who had apparently been sleeping, stood up and shuffled a few steps to the door. Huffing, the man pushed back an iron bolt and lumbered to move the giant door. *What is this, a castle? Where's the drawbridge?*

Light filled the space, illuminating the short, yawning porter in a black *djellaba*.

"*Monsieur*," the Moroccan said, extending his hand.

He wants a tip for that? Dylan rustled in his pocket for some coins, gave the porter what he had, and stepped into the morning air. *Might as well, he saved my ass.*

"*Merci*," the man said before yawning, waving as Dylan set

4

off down the narrow alley.

The labyrinthine neighborhood behind Marrakech's main square—the Djema el-Fna—intimidated Dylan during his one night in the city. He remembered to walk straight and turn right at the corner shop, but he forgot the way from there. *Kayla could always remember directions like that as if she had a built-in compass. Move on, Dyl—she wasn't always right.*

Approaching a three-way junction, he looked left and right, but he recognized neither. To the left, an orange cat ate something in the alley, but the right appeared darker. He looked at the phone: 6:34. "*The bus leaves at seven*," Lily had said. Dylan felt warm with his long-sleeve shirt and heavy pack. *Quick, decide. Left.* He walked toward the cat.

Startled, the cat retreated to an open door where an unwashed boy, perhaps nine years old, sat on a step playing with an empty sardine can. The filthy cat brushed against him, longing for attention. Trash littered the threshold and the place smelled of urine. Seeing Dylan, the boy looked up at him, smiled, and stuck out his hand.

"Er, *pardon, mani taxi?*" Dylan stumbled in a mix of French and the Berber dialect of Tashelheet he studied in training.

"*Stylu, s'il vous plaît?*" the boy asked with his hand outstretched. A young woman with a baby emerged from the shadows of the house. She said nothing but looked at Dylan.

Dylan paused before responding to the boy, not expecting the woman. *She's young. And tired. And thin.* He continued to look at her—she was close to his age—and then he stared at the baby in her arms. He struggled to swallow. *Her brown eyes are wide, like Kayla's. Pretty.* He turned his attention back to the boy.

"No, I don't have a pen to give you. Please, the taxi?"

The boy pointed back from where Dylan had come. The

woman said nothing.

"*Shukran*," he said, thanking the boy.

"*Stylu, s'il vous plaît?*" he repeated with his hand still out-stretched. Dylan shook his head, turned, and hastily walked back down the alley, but felt no more confident in his decision. He looked back at the impoverished scene: the woman, the boy with the rusty sardine can, the soiled cat, and the squalor. *Horror.*

Retracing his steps, he soon faced another intersection. The right looked slightly dark; the left looked a little brighter. "*Follow the light,*" he heard his saintly grandmother say in his head—the thought of her made him smile. He went to the left which emptied onto a street with parked cars. *No taxis.* The phone read 6:46. *Fuck. The square must be over there,* he looked right and started to walk, passing a closet-like patisserie. The smell of fresh bread teased him in the street, reminding him of his morning hunger. *No time*, he told himself, and continued on. A car cut across the street ahead. *A stop sign. I'll wait here. Something will pass soon enough.* He waited only a minute, shifting his weight from foot to foot.

"*Bonjour*," the driver said as he leaned out of the window. Dylan struggled to get the pack off his back and into the small beige Renault. He felt the wet shirt cling to his back. Dylan sweated when he got nervous, even on a cool morning like this.

"*Où voulez-vous aller, mon ami?*"

"Er, bus?" he faltered, not knowing French and only weak Arabic. He only had the little Tashelheet he learned in training as a crutch. Dylan struggled with Latin in high school and college, so parsing French while under pressure daunted him.

The driver looked confusedly at him.

Shit—what's this? Kayla knew French, but she'd be useless here.

6

Figure it out, the bus is gonna roll.

During training, he had a language class dedicated to transportation words, but in his panic, he failed to recall any of them. *Gare means station—but is that for the bus or train?* He reached into his pocket and pulled out the folded paper with directions. He held the photograph while, frantically, he scanned the words:

CATCH 7 AM CTM BUS NEAR SOUQ FOR OUARZAZATE, THEN
TRANSFER TO KELAA

"C-T-M. *Souq*," he shouted. In the mirror, the driver appeared confused before his eyes widened.

"CTM. *Souq. Wa-ha*," the driver repeated, turning the key in the ignition and heading down the street. "CTM. *Mezyan*." Dylan recognized *mezyan* as the word the language tutors said to the smart kids in class. He figured it meant something like "very good," and he cracked a smile. He folded the paper again along its sharp creases and slipped it with the photograph back into his pocket, exchanging them for his phone. 6:53. *Fuck.*

Dylan had arrived in Marrakech by bus from Fez, but he was unsure how far he had to travel to return to the station. Seven minutes seemed a short amount of time to get there, regardless. Beads of sweat formed on his forehead and the car lacked a crank to roll down the passenger window. *They never open the windows in cars, they told us that in training*, he remembered. He stared through the window. Although he had wandered in the cramped old alleys around the Djema el-Fna the evening before, he found that the French-style avenues and boulevards in this part of the city gave a modern exterior to medieval Marrakech. Billboards proudly showed pictures of King Muhammad VI and an abundance of lifeless Moroccan flags on that still morning. *Who'd have thought I'd be in Marrakech? At twenty-three? Working? Well, volunteering. This will be great.*

7

On his right, he saw a solitary teenage boy with a thin, three-legged dog walking through an empty lot, with buses parked on the far side. *Not far, just over there.* He looked back at the boy with the sickly dog as the taxi whizzed past. *What will he do today? What does he do any day? Kayla would hate this place—she hated anything that wouldn't get her to law school. Almost cruel.* Before pursuing the thought further, he turned his attention back to the phone, which read 6:58, and could feel the taxi slow. The driver entered the depot and Dylan jumped onto the curb with his pack, now focused on finding the Ouarzazate bus.

"*Chal?*" Dylan asked, looking into the driver's rolled-down window at the meter: it was turned off. The meter had not calculated his fare. *You've got to be fucking kidding me. They said this would happen in training. I forgot to have him turn it on.*

"*Cinquante,*" the driver said as he calmly extended his left hand. Dylan rolled his eyes. He had confidence in his Arabic numbers but hated person-to-person confrontation.

"*Eshra?*" His nervous and dry voice cracked when he suggested ten dirhams.

"*Hamseen,*" the driver still insisted fifty. Dylan had little experience of Moroccan taxi drivers, but he knew the five-minute ride was not worth fifty dirhams.

"*Eshreen,*" he said giving the man a purple twenty dirham note. Dylan grabbed his pack and turned away, letting the man's shouts—and the horn of his taxi—blend with the rest of the noise of the street behind. Taking in a deep breath as he adjusted the weight of the pack on his back, he again cracked a smile. *It's ok, I got this. I do.*

The depot bustled. On the left stood a dozen or so CTM-emblazoned buses, but they appeared locked with no activity around them. On the opposite side, with much more excitement, older buses with scratched paint and cracked windshields lined the lot. There, men carried crates of goods while women balanced bundles on their heads and kids in their arms. *Mother of God, they have to carry kids with that shit on top of their heads?* Boys hoisted the bundles and sacks onto the bus roof. *No time for the zoo today.*

Lily gave him clear instructions: *Take the CTM bus at seven for Ouarzazate and pronounce the city's name as War-za-zat.* His phone read 7:03, but the engines stood silently and none had left the lot while he stood there. *It's ok, I made it,* he reassured himself.

"Ouarzazate?" He asked a man carrying boxes tied with string. The man walked on.

"Ouarzazate?" He questioned a uniformed man leaning against a CTM bus. The driver lit a cigarette, inspected Dylan from head to toe, and pointed across the lot to the older buses. "CTM *sa* Ouarzazate, *si'l vous plaît.*" Dylan tried with his smattering of languages.

"*C'est là-bas,*" the man said, still pointing to the activity near the last bus in the row. As Dylan turned to look, the driver took his cigarette into the bus and closed the door.

Lily said CTM. These buses all say CTM. They told me to avoid souq buses in training, he thought as he walked across the pavement. CTM, the national bus line, kept set schedules, fixed prices, and drove more modern vehicles. The older souq buses made frequent unscheduled stops and connected markets—*souqs*—set apart from one another. Dylan approached the mass of people.

"*Pardon,* Ouarzazate?" Dylan addressed the swarm around the bus. No one paid him any attention as they stored their myriad belongings. Through the cracked windshield, he could see two ladies sitting in the front seat holding handkerchiefs in front of their mouths. The driver, in his seat, wiped the interior of the windshield with a dirty cloth, smudging it more than cleaning it, and talked to another middle-aged man who stood next to him. A younger man, probably the same age as Dylan and wearing a faded Coca-Cola t-shirt, arranged the cargo in the hold below. *Suitcases go underneath, everything else on top of the roof. I wonder why?* Dirty, stray dogs sniffed the people milling about.

Dylan stood motionless near the door, unsure of what to do. The young man in the Coca-Cola t-shirt reached for the pack on Dylan's back and Dylan pulled back in surprise.

"*Y'allah, monsieur.*" The young man's urgency suggested it was time to go.

"To Ouarzazate?" Dylan asked. "CTM?"

"Are you American?"

"Yes," Dylan replied.

"Yes, we go to Ouarzazate, if you hurry up. Give me your bag. *Y'allah.*"

"Is this the CTM bus?" Dylan probed, confused.

"There is no morning CTM to Ouarzazate. *Souq* bus only."

This doesn't make sense. Lily said CTM at seven. What other choice do I have, though? He took off his pack. "*Wa-ha,*" Dylan consented.

"*Wa-ha?* You speak Moroccan?"

"*Shwiya,*" Dylan replied, confessing his limited vocabulary.

"*Mezyan, mezyan.*" The young man hurried Dylan toward the bus door where the man—speaking to the driver—stood, holding a fist full of small papers.

"*Billet, monsieur?*" the man asked without turning from the driver.

Billet. Billet. What is billet? Dylan shrugged his shoulders. A woman in a *hijab*, holding a toddler by the hand, squeezed past Dylan and sat in the second row of the bus. Both the driver and the other man ignored the woman as she greeted them.

"Ur sinugh," he shrugged his shoulders. Dylan knew how to profess ignorance in Tashelheet, having used the phrase many times during training. He also knew he stood a good distance away from Berber country in urban Marrakech. Turning to Dylan, the man grinned and looked back at the driver.

"Ur sinugh?" The men chuckled and the driver examined Dylan.

"You need ticket, *monsieur. Billet,*" the driver said. His old, dirty khaki coat read "STAFF" over the left breast.

"Wa-ha, chal?" Dylan asked how much while nodding.

"Timeneen," the collector said. Dylan reached for a brown hundred dirham note—he only had two left—and handed it to the collector, who returned twenty dirhams in change. *"Wa-ha,"* and the man stressed *"billet"* while raising it for Dylan to see.

"Billet," Dylan repeated, committing the word to memory.

"You go to Ouarzazate?" the driver interrupted in English.

"Ouarzazate then Boumalne Dades," Dylan said with a nod.

"No," the driver said, shaking his head. "It is not possible."

You've got to be fucking kidding me.

"First Ouarzazate, then Kelaa', then Boumalne Dades. This is the only way," the driver said as he continued to shake both his head and his finger at Dylan.

"Wa-ha. Shukran," Dylan agreed and recalled Lily's instructions. He remembered her insistence to *"arrive by four, no later."* His dry throat burned as he looked for a seat. *Only eight more hours to go,* he calculated. *What's the worst that could happen? I spend the night in Boumalne?* He remembered what Lily had said: *"Trust me, you don't want to get stuck there."* *I'll make it.*

People filled only three-fourths of the seats in the dark, stuffy bus with shut windows. He chose an empty seat toward the back, just in front of a balding middle-aged man wearing an old sport coat and an Oxford shirt. The man gave Dylan a nod but said nothing. Dylan returned the nod before he sat down, sliding toward the window. *Useless to try to open it, they'll just make me shut it again. What is it with the windows?*

A goat bleated.

Slowly, he turned and saw at the very rear a black goat with its elderly owner.

Of course. Of fucking course. Why not bring a goat on a bus? he asked himself as he returned to look out the dirty window. He shook his head in annoyance, but then blurted out a laugh. *A goat on a bus—with an old guy—is fucking hilarious*, he reminded himself. *Kayla would fucking hate that. Glad she's not here. I guess.* Outside, a heavy rope hung loosely across his window but then disappeared, used to secure the last of the roof-top goods. Dylan watched the young man in the Coke t-shirt jump down, walk to the bus door, step inside, and close it.

"Y'*allah,*" the young man said with a clap, giving the signal to the driver to depart. After a couple of honest efforts, the engine turned over and a thick cloud of black exhaust billowed from the rear and the smell of diesel filled the cabin. The driver honked his horn six times and the beast lurched forward, almost an hour after Dylan expected to embark. Through the smudged window, he saw a gatekeeper in a blue coat swing open a metal bar that served as a barrier and, in turn, salute the bus as it passed. Feeling more at ease, Dylan smiled at the man and waved as the bus gained speed. Even though he knew it was now after eight, he instinctively reached for his phone but stopped himself. *I can't miss my connection on the first day, they'll never take me seriously. I've got to make this work.* He felt the phone from outside his pocket, reminding himself it rested there with the picture of Kayla and his sister. *I'm doing it, the adventure continues* he reassured himself, and continued to look ahead to the new world beyond the bus.

Dylan rested his head on the vinyl seatback and again unfolded the paper from his pocket. Lily's instructions plainly said CTM bus, but despite the changes, he had solved the problem. *This is fucking great. Really, it is.* The next instruction read:

IN OUARZAZATE, EXIT TERMINAL, USE TOILET
AND CROSS STREET TO TAXIS. ASK FOR KELAA

Pee, cross, street, taxi to Kelaa', no problem. I wonder, though, why I can't go directly to Boumalne? Before putting the paper back in his pocket, he unfolded the photograph. *Aly's asleep at home this early. Is Kayla asleep, and alone?* he wondered regretfully. He noticed her brown eyes before slipping the picture back in his pocket. Only fifteen minutes into the trip and the boy with the young mother near the front of the bus fussed. *Poor girl, all alone with that kid. I'm glad I'm not sitting up there, though.*

The shadows cast by the few palm trees that lined the Marrakech road occasionally broke the glare of the strong sun. As they crossed the city limits and headed south toward the mountains, they passed some recently-built apartments over ground-level *hanoots:* shops, pharmacies, and grocers. *Marrakech suburbs.* A few pockets of poverty appeared here and there as warrens of corrugated metal, but most of the multi-story construction appeared new. *There are nice apartments and abandoned lots with burning rubbish. At home, we keep that stuff separate, here it's all mixed together. Developers could do wonders here with just a little cash.*

As an hour turned to two and one small roadside village blended with another, Dylan focused his thoughts inward. *The small hanoots all sell the same things—packets of biscuits, bags of chips, cartons of soap, bottles of soda. Only sometimes do you see crates of melons or oranges. Everything advertises Coca-Cola, or sometimes Fanta. It all feels the same and mass-produced.* His breath had slowed and he felt more comfortable. *But I'm here now. I'm doing it, and this is great.* He looked at the phone, this time noticing the date rather than the hour. *September 14. Shit. Mom's birthday. Not sure when I'll call. She'll be ok, she remembers what it's like.* In his mind, he returned to his parents' garage the November before. His father stored the fall rakes while his mother swept the floor in their winter preparations. Dylan stood in the open garage door with the late-autumn wind at his back.

"*Peace Corps, Dyl? Where'd that come from?*" she had asked.

"*I thought you and Dad would be happy. You two met in the Peace Corps for God's sake! I figured you expected it from me.*"

"*We didn't expect it Dyl, it's just a big surprise. But we're happy, very happy, aren't we Diane?*" his father had said.

"*Of course we are. It just seems a little soon, you know, since Kayla and the wedding.*"

"*It's been a year, Ma. And I didn't know what else to do.*"

"*You're not running away, are you? Not escaping? Things haven't been the same since Kay...*" she tried to console him, but his father interrupted.

"*Drop it, Di. Where are you going, Dyl?*"

"*Tom, I am letting him be. I'm just surprised. I want to make sure it's the right decision.*"

"*I'm going to Morocco, Dad. Kayla just wanted to focus on law school. People change. People make different decisions. Sometimes bad decisions. It's fine, really. I'm over it.*"

14

"*It'll be good for him, Diane. And Morocco! That's better than fine, Dyl. That's great, although not at all like Ghana, I'm sure. We'll have to plan a trip. Have you told your sister yet?*"

"*No, not yet. You're first, Dad.*"

"*Morocco, Dylan? Are you sure?*" she asked, motherly.

"*Yes, he's sure Di. It's the great adventure.*"

"*That's what you always called it, Tom. Graduate school would be a greater one.*"

"*It's great, Di. It was great for us and it'll be great for him. This is just what you need to move on and get back on track, Dyl. You've been lost for the last year.*"

"*When do you leave?*" she pressed.

"*June 24. I'll keep working construction until then. I'll save some money to travel while I'm away. It'll be good, Ma. I'm excited.*"

"*It will be good, Dylan. I am happy for you. I'm sorry I mentioned Kayla. I'm sure it's still sensitive. I just want to be sure you're going for the right reasons. I wouldn't be a good mom if I didn't.*"

"*It's ok, Ma. Really. I'm not running. I'm over her. I got this.*"

He found himself again staring at and talking to Kayla in the picture as he sat on the rumbling bus. *Life is different now, for me and for you.* He looked at her smile and noticed the light freckle on her cheek. *I miss you. I'm also still fucking pissed at you.* The bus hit a pothole and broke his memory as he put the picture back into his pocket. *This is good—no, great.*

The bus sounded relatively quiet despite having thirty-or-so people and a goat on-board. The young man in the Coke t-shirt silently stood at the front of the bus while the ticket collector sat behind the driver and the two older men talked. The young woman still struggled with her fussy toddler near the front. *Thank God they're not sitting near me. And thank God there are no other children.* But there were bundles! In addition to the

15

packages tied to the roof and the luggage underneath, everyone had bundles of things: jugs of oil, boxes of dates, baguettes, and big plastic bags stuffed with colorful heavy blankets; as if an entire caravan had been packed-up and fit into the bus. *Without camels*, Dylan thought and again looked back at the goat. This time, the old man waved and smiled toothlessly. Dylan nodded and turned back around, sinking into his seat and pulling his cap over his eyes.

He sat impatiently; this exciting world opened before him and he could not rest. The terrain grew hilly and a sandy rock-strewn ground dotted with small evergreens replaced the red dirt of Marrakech. The road wound more tightly around cliffs as they climbed into the mountains. The pleasant country-side—perhaps like the western part of the United States Dylan had never seen—looked quite unlike the green hills of his native western Massachusetts. He had spent a lot of time in those hills, especially in college. The picture he kept in his pocket came from the summit of Mount Greylock two summers before. *That was a perfect day!* He remembered. *I decided to propose without a ring, and I asked her the next morning before we got out of bed.*

"Of course, Dyl," she had said, before hesitating. *"Wait. What about law school? I figured we'd wait until after I finished law school. It sounds great, but I just don't know."*

"Go to law school, Kay! I want you to go. We'll make it work."

"You think? It's going to be intense."

"Would you rather do it on your own or with me taking care of you? Billions of people are married. And plenty of people go to law school. How hard can it be?"

"Yup, you're right. I'm ready. I've been ready all year. Let's do it," she said before kissing him.

We stayed in bed all morning. It was amazing. No, it was

16

beautiful, actually. Life made more sense then—before it went to shit. Wish that had worked. Now I've got to make this work. He again looked at his phone to see that it read 9:12.

The bus took increasingly-sharper turns as it growled higher into the mountains. The goat, while remaining tethered to its master, became animated in the confined space. *Just don't look back there*, he told himself staring forward. Ahead, a long baguette poked out from the top of a woman's shopping bag. Another woman, seated behind the baguette, broke off a bit and began to eat. *Are they traveling together or is this just what you do on long bus rides?* Across the aisle, an old Berber woman—her tattooed face revealed her native heritage—sat hunched over, holding a small empty plastic shopping bag in her hands. *I really hope she's not going to be sick.* The driver continued to shift gears as the bus climbed upward. *Why won't that kid in the Coke shirt sit? There's plenty of empty seats.*

Winding curves and the steep incline made the journey slow. Often the bus would stop to allow oncoming cars to pass in the one-lane road. No passengers disembarked in the mountains. No guardrail protected them from the lethal cliff edges. Dylan noticed his heartbeat steadily increase over the last hour: the smell of bus exhaust, the goat, and the seemingly ever-present danger just outside made him curious. Looking out of the cracked windshield ahead, beyond the woman and her toddler, beyond the driver and the other men, he saw the mountain crest. They had reached the summit. Dylan took another deep breath as he surveyed the unimaginable scene before him. The mountains undulated until they disappeared in the purple haze of the horizon. The road hugged the cliff edge and below he could see cars and vans maneuver up and down the slope. He could only glimpse the verdant valley far below from the window. The green, solitary ribbon wound through the russet ground. *I didn't expect this*, he said to himself. *New England mountains are so green, these are so very different. Boumalne is somewhere past those mountains, I think, in the desert. There's no way I can get there by four. But there's only one ride to the village each afternoon; I've got to make it.*

The downhill journey passed more quickly than the ascent, and the bus felt like an old wooden rollercoaster. The woman across the aisle sank lower into her seat while her grip never relaxed its hold of the plastic bag. Dylan, too, became nauseous as the bleating of the goat reverberated in his head. When the driver took a sharp turn and the bus rocked, Dylan grabbed hold of the seat in front of him. *I need a break, this has got to stop.* Just then, the old woman vomited forcefully into her thin plastic bag. The smell quickly filled the enclosed space of the bus. Other women, seated nearby, came to her aid, handing her tissues and rubbing her back. Someone tied the plastic bag and passed it, along with its contents, to the front of the bus where the boy in the Coke t-shirt threw it out of the bus door. *This is a nightmare.*

"The old ladies, they get sick." Dylan heard a voice behind him say as he turned to look at the man in the sport coat. "They do not travel. Where are you going? The Ouarzazate road is not often traveled by visitors."

"I am going to live near Ouarzazate," Dylan said confidently.

"Live there? Are you making a film? Are you Italian?"

"No, American. I will work in a village clinic for two years."

"A young American doctor. This is very good. The people there need your help. There are many problems, many problems, in the desert."

"I'm not a doctor. Just a volunteer. Peace Corps."

"Ah, Peace Corps," he pronounced the "s" in Corps even though Dylan had not. "I know Peace Corps. They are very good. My first English teacher was Peace Corps. He was a very nice man named Michael. Very good work. America and Morocco are very good friends. I am Hamid," he said, extending his hand over the dividing seat.

"I am Yusuf, *metsharfin*," Dylan said, indicating that it was nice to meet him.

"*Metsharfin*. How is your Arabic, then?" Hamid asked.

"I learned Tashelheet and very little Arabic," Dylan confessed.

"Tashelheet! I do not speak Berber. They are good people with a strange language."

"It seems," Dylan said, betraying a smile.

Dylan passed time talking to Hamid, but the conversation remained shallow: a few details about Hamid's life in the coastal city of Agadir, but he skirted questions about employment and his business in Ouarzazate. Uninterested, Dylan left it alone.

"May I ask, Yusuf, why did you become Peace Corps?"

"My parents had been in the Peace Corps in Ghana, but I didn't have any good plans after college. I applied, they accepted me, and now I'm here. It's not a very exciting story, I'm afraid." Dylan blushed a little.

"You have such opportunities in America. For the few of us who go to university in Morocco, we work hard to find good jobs here. They are few," Hamid said shaking his head with a sense of disappointment. "What did you study, Yusuf?"

"Economics. Not to get rich. I guess to try to help the poor. I suppose that's why I joined the Peace Corps—to help people. You went to university, Hamid?"

"I did. I studied English literature. Dickens is my favorite—such rich novels."

19

"Yes, I like Dickens, too, especially *Great Expectations.*"

"Ah, yes, *Great Expectations.* Young Pip. And Estella, his love. Where is your Estella, Yusuf?" he said with a laugh.

"I don't have one. Where is yours?" Dylan fired back; he felt his face become warmer. "It is good," he said awkwardly after a pause, afraid he had insulted the stranger.

"She is at home in Agadir. It is good, *mashi mushkil*, Yusuf" Hamid replied, finding no problem. They both turned their attention back out the window.

When they reached the valley floor, Dylan saw small buildings dot the road with signs that read "TOURIST" and "COCA-COLA." The bus slowed and sounded its horn, alerting the villagers of the hamlet of their arrival. Rather than fight the disembarking crowd, Dylan waited to leave after the others. He glanced at the rear of the bus. *The fucking goat is staying. Fantastic.*

"You go, Yusuf. I am staying on the bus," Hamid said as Dylan stood to walk out. The women walked in pairs, like nuns, across the street toward the *hanoots,* but Dylan could not see the woman with the querulous toddler.

Nearby, a shopkeeper roasted kebabs making the mountain air smoky. Beside the grill, a butcher hung carcasses in the morning sun. Flies swarmed around the meat. *The goat on the bus is next.* He walked across the street where a small middle-aged man wiped white plastic tables and chairs to entice weary travelers to his café with its "Nescafé" sign. A painted blue arrow with "WC" directed Dylan to a dark room in the back of the building.

He fastened the bolt on the toilet door, but it did not seem secure. The toilet smelled foul and none of the other passengers waited to use it. Dylan decided not to linger. His gut felt uncomfortable; the traveler's money belt he wore cut into his stomach. He unfastened it and stuffed it into his pocket. *Who is*

20

going to mug me here? A thief wouldn't get anything anyway, there aren't many dirhams left. How far could he get with my passport? When he finished, he looked to wash his hands, but the closet lacked a sink. *I have hand sanitizer on the bus,* he thought. *Well, under the bus. Useless.* He sighed and unlatched the sticky bolt.

In the sunlight, Dylan looked at his phone: 11:06. *I need to eat.* A small *hanoot* next to the café sold dusty bags of potato chips, packets of biscuits, and warm bottles of orange Fanta. *Always Fanta or Coke, never water. My bottle is with the hand sanitizer.* The dirty packages of the bare shop did not appeal to Dylan while the roasting kebabs across the way again caught his attention. *Goat at eleven in the morning? Could be worse, I guess.* He crossed the traffic-less road to the small grill where the young man in the Coke t-shirt stood.

"*Salamu alaykum,*" Dylan greeted the cook who barely acknowledged him in return.

"Hello," the young man said while chewing.

"*Tleta, afak,*" Dylan said, raising three fingers. The man shook his head to indicate no. Dylan paused. *I know tleta means three in Arabic. Maybe he only knows Tashelheet.* "*Shrad,*" Dylan tried, again raising three fingers, this time with more conviction. The man at the grill looked up and again shook his head no, glancing at the butcher next door. The guy in the Coke t-shirt—who chewed on a skewer of kebabs—looked at Dylan.

"You must buy the meat from his brother—there—then he will cook it here."

"*Shukran,*" Dylan responded and the young man nodded. Dylan walked over to the butcher and saw the raw meat hanging in the open air. A severed sheep's head lay on the blood-stained tile counter with its stiff tongue exposed in the open mouth. *There's a goat on the bus.* He turned back to cross the road. *Fanta and chips will do.*

Dylan watched the young man in the Coke t-shirt, unsure how long the rest stop would last. After munching his chips and sipping his warm Fanta, Dylan enjoyed stretching in the sunlight despite breathing in the smells of smoke and meat. *Even with the barbecue, it still smells better than Marrakech.* Near the bus, the young mother stood in the shade holding her ornery toddler by the hand. *She must be about my age, and the kid must be four. Wow. A mother at eighteen. Why is she traveling alone?* The woman wore mismatched clothes—a dark green *hijab* around her face, a black shirt, and a long blue denim skirt. The boy had brown corduroy pants and a grey sweater. *He must be warm, even in the shade there. Probably hungry, too because they're not eating anything. They look miserable.* Dylan felt some coins in his pocket and looked back at the dusty *hanoot* where he bought his lunch. *Biscuits and Fanta.* Instead of taking out the dirhams, he looked at his phone again to see that it was 11:21. He looked up from his phone and back at the woman and child, putting the phone back in his pocket. *Do it. Coward.* He heard the bus driver start the engine and give six loud honks of the horn. Tossing his trash in a cardboard box nearby, Dylan crossed the empty street and resumed his seat, passing the woman and the child. The driver did not wait long, nor did he count to see if everyone had returned to the bus. Dylan glanced at the rear of the bus; the goat had remained where he left it and the old man again smiled and waved. *Christ. Why are you here?*

The second leg of the journey passed much like the first, although Dylan now knew what to expect. The old woman across the aisle kept her head in her lap but never again vomited. As the bus climbed out of the valley, the terrain changed. To the south, the land stretched as an endlessly flat desert. In his short three months in Morocco, Dylan had enjoyed seeing different parts of the kingdom: the manmade lake of Azilal, the monkey forests of Ifrane, the seaport of Essaouira, and the ancient cities of Fez and Meknes. But here lay the great desert he had longed to see and where he would make his home for the next two years. The work before him seemed surprisingly undefined: his job description read "health educator" and, despite his training, he had only a basic understanding that he should "teach people to be healthy." He would determine the methods to use to achieve that goal in the village when he arrived. *How can you help a whole village when you can't help a woman and a tiny kid?*

Dylan looked at the people around him. Almost all of the women had their heads covered with colored scarves, and like the men, some wore western-style clothes and others wore *djellabas*. No one appeared particularly flashy in their appearance. *I'm not sure if they're very different from the people back home or just like them. Their clothes and language are different, but these seem to be honest people going about their business in a different corner of the world. The women who helped the sick lady were probably more willing than women in the US. The driver and the ticket collector talk and laugh just as they would back home.* The young man in the Coke t-shirt remained a mystery to Dylan. *Why doesn't he sit or talk to anyone? He only stares outside. He knows decent English, but what's his future as a bus porter? He's got to be my age. What the hell is my future?* Dylan's thoughts were interrupted when the goat bleated and its owner shushed it; shaking his head in annoyance, Dylan shut his eyes to rest.

What was my future after Williams? Yeah, we were going to get married, but I didn't have plans—grad school, law school, or teaching—I still don't know. When Kayla shattered everything, I just fell into this, and now I'm here. Getting into Peace Corps was pretty simple; the essays were a joke and I easily passed the physical. But now that I'm here, I've got to make this work—no, I want to make this work, he repeated to himself as the bus descended from the mountains. *There's nothing left back home.*

Ouarzazate remains a desert city—not the sandy dunes depicted by Hollywood, but a monotonous hamada that extends south from the Atlases. The bus entered a roundabout with an empty fountain. Like elsewhere in Morocco, the buildings—all painted rose—stood no higher than three stories, with *hanoots* at street-level and apartments above. *It's more compact than Pittsfield, but probably has just as many people,* he figured. *So many abandoned lots and so much litter. The dogs always look so sickly,* he thought, cringing, as a boy outside threw a stone at an emaciated mutt. Dylan had no fondness for animals, especially dogs, but he pitied the feral ones. He reached for the picture again but stopped. His eye noticed the young mother at the front of the bus struggling with her unhappy boy. *Poor girl. So different from Kayla.*

The bus entered the comparatively quiet depot and everyone hastily disembarked.

"*Bon chance*, Yusuf," Hamid said as they gathered their things. "May your work here be good, like David Copperfield."

"*Shukran*. Yes, I guess like David Copperfield" Dylan said as he extended his hand for Hamid's. *Copperfield was a writer, and I'm not—but wasn't it the second wife that he really loved?* They exchanged nods before turning to leave the old bus. Dylan scanned the passengers for the young woman and child. *They've got to be hungry. I'll give them dirhams this time.*

Outside, the passengers crowded around the porter while he unpacked the cargo-hold, forming a mob rather than a line. Dylan looked among the crowd for the woman and boy but could not find them. His pack, however, appeared unmistakable amid the second-hand suitcases and bags. He hurriedly gave the young man ten dirhams for his effort.

"*Shukran,*" the young man thanked Dylan. "You knows where to go?"

"Yes. To the grand taxis?" Dylan asked. The porter pointed toward the gate and the line of old Mercedes across the street.

"*Wa-ha. Shukran. B'slama,*" Dylan said.

"*B'slama.* Good luck, my friend," replied the young man as he slipped the coin into his back pocket and ducked back into the cargo hold.

He called me his friend.

Dylan awkwardly lifted his heavy pack as the people moved around him, but the woman and her boy had vanished. *I missed my second chance. Idiot.* Once free from the crowd, he hoisted the pack onto his back and set off across the quiet pavement. *Lily said to pee, but it's almost two. I don't really have to use the toilet, I just need to get to Boumalne. I'll piss there.*

"*Marraksh, Marraksh, Marraksh,*" a driver called while sitting on the hood of his Mercedes. *Nope, I don't want to go back to Marrakech, thank you very much,* he thought as he walked through the taxi stand. There were a dozen or so similar drivers with their taxis, each waiting for the requisite number of six passengers before they would begin their onward journeys. Some had presumably been waiting for hours to find six passengers. Dylan knew how the system worked. *Got to make it by four.*

"*Où?*" a dark-skinned man in a dirty blue turban asked Dylan where he wanted to go. His uneven mustache revealed a missing front tooth when he smiled.

"Boumalne Dades," Dylan replied confidently.

"No," the man said, shaking a finger. "Kelaa' M'Gouna..." and proceeded to speak in Arabic until Dylan interrupted him.

"Tashelheet?"

The man stopped, perplexed that Dylan wanted to speak Berber. He repeated "Tashelheet" to his friends, and they laughed. "*Wa-ha*. Tashelheet," he said and explained that Dylan would first have to go to Kelaa' and then catch a ride to Boumalne. Both Lily and the bus driver had already explained this to Dylan, but he hoped to find a direct ride.

"*Y'allah*. Kelaa'," said a thin man with extra large pants who lifted Dylan's pack from his shoulders and the assembled group of onlookers—whose objective seemed only to stand in the lot—followed the man in the turban to a waiting taxi.

"*Y'allah, y'allah,*" the man with the turban said to the driver who sat on the hood of his old beige Mercedes. Three middle-aged men and an old *hajj* conversed behind the taxi and moved toward the car; counting Dylan they had five passengers. The man with the big pants struggled to stuff Dylan's pack in the trunk, but it would not fit with the other luggage.

"*Mashi mushkil,*" the driver said, searching the trunk for rope.

They never see anything as a problem here. The assembled helped strap the pack to the roof of the Mercedes. Dylan watched. *That better make it to Kelaa' or I'm screwed.* The man in the blue turban extended his hand.

"*Vingt-huit.*"

Vingt means twenty, but I don't know huit. I'll give him thirty, Dylan thought as he fumbled with the bills and coins. The man returned two dirham coins before walking away.

"*Shukran,*" Dylan said.

"*Bla jmil,*" the man responded without looking back.

The other passengers began positioning themselves for the

ride to Kelaa'. Customarily, four of them would sit in the back seat while two would squeeze into the front passenger's seat. Dylan again counted the group and, with himself, they still only numbered five. Hoping for a spacious ride in the front, Dylan opened the passenger door amid shouts of "no, no, no!" When he looked in, he saw the sixth passenger, a pretty woman of about twenty wearing a pink *djellaba* with her head wrapped in a fashionable matching *hijab*.

I can't sit next to her, Dylan thought as he froze, having learned about gender customs in training, *she'll freak out. How much impropriety could happen in a taxi with seven people?* He smirked at his own thought. *Still, pointless to argue.*

"*Samhi*," Dylan apologized stepping back. *No one responded so I guess it was a mushkil.*

The four men and Dylan stood while the driver tightened the rope to secure the pack. The elderly man who held a stuffed plastic bag stepped toward the passenger door. In their conversation, the men had decided that the *hajj*, who wore a maroon *djellaba* and a small white knitted cap, posed the least threat to the girl. The others miserably stuffed themselves into the rear seat and generously allowed Dylan to sit on the end, working hard to situate themselves as best they could. The driver jumped in his seat, invoked Divine favor on the journey by saying "*Bismillah*," and turned the key. The engine sputtered and lurched as they departed. Out of habit, Dylan reached for his phone to check the time but could not reach the phone, encumbered by the seating arrangement. The four men in the rear were especially cramped since the man wedged next to Dylan measured twice his size.

The taxi soon reached the city limits of Ouarzazate. Beyond unfolded that same dry, empty terrain Dylan saw on his descent from the Atlases. Two of the men talked with each other while everyone else remained silent. The driver played a cassette of traditional Moroccan music; Dylan disliked the repetitive, ululating style but had grown accustomed to it during training. He focused on all that lay before him.

Distant stony hills made something of a corridor as they traveled along the smooth two-lane Highway N10. *Empty. Like when Luke Skywalker looked to the horizon on that desert planet. Just empty. Saturday nights watching Star Wars—sweet memories with Kay.* He saw three camels amble in the distance. *I wonder where they're going? Is anyone with them?* Closer to the road, a teenage girl tended a herd of scruffy goats while yet another apparently starving dog trailed behind. All the figures in the scene were tiny in comparison to the immensity of the vista that opened wide before them. The girl held a small piece of flimsy cardboard over her head to block the strong sun. Dylan looked at her. *She's in Hell. What future does she have with goats, in the desert? I want to help her—well, not her, but a girl like her. Kayla and Aly have every chance, what chance does she have? Kayla had every fucking chance. Still, you're here and she's not. Do this.* The hard vinyl of the taxi door pressed against Dylan's side. *It's all over if this opens*, he thought. Rarely did he pray, but said a *Hail Mary* to feel safe—surprising himself with his devotion.

More rose-colored concrete buildings dotted the roadside as they approached a village. Electrical poles, made from poured cement, followed the road and reminded Dylan that the "developed" world existed alongside the "developing." The stretch of road became bordered by bushes and small irrigated green fields.

"*Mani?*" Dylan asked where they were, hoping someone understood his Tashelheet.

"Kelaa'," the man next to him said, "*des roses*," and pointed out the window reaching across Dylan's chest. "*La fête du sud.*" Dylan nodded to acknowledge him. Lily had mentioned the famed rose bushes of Kelaa' at their meeting. *I must be close.*

"*Azigzaw.* Green," Dylan said haltingly, as he commented on the color of the field.

"*Azigzaw,*" the man repeated with a laugh, "*azigzaw.*"

I should say more, Dylan thought as he contorted a smile. *He wants to talk, but I'm not good at these conversations. Peace Corps says I'm supposed to be making friendships, but I'm not.* The large man again repeated "*azigzaw,*" nodding. *I suck at this,* Dylan thought to return the nod.

For such a small town, it's a lot busier than Ouarzazate, he thought. While there had been a dozen waiting taxis in Ouarzazate, only two waited in Kelaa'. *One of these better be fucking going to Boumalne*, he said under his breath as he stepped out and stretched his neck and spine. He looked at his phone—2:48—and switched it off. Then he turned it back on again and re-read the time. Still 2:48. *Just want to be sure.* The driver unpacked the trunk first and only attended to Dylan's rooftop pack after the others had dispersed. No one approached Dylan to ask him where he was going, so he asked the driver when he received his pack.

"*Mani taxi sa Boumalne?*" Dylan asked in Tashelheet.

The driver shrugged his shoulders and walked over to a group of men standing on the small curb. Frustrated, Dylan looked around to try to make sense of his situation. *Is it my language or me?* Behind him, he saw a busy street with a bank and post office. *Both are useless*, he thought. To his right was a small vegetable market and to his left was a café with white plastic tables and chairs. He watched the driver talk to the small group of men and point at Dylan, prompting one of the men to approach him.

"Good afternoon, sir. You would like to go to Boumalne? I can take you."

Finding both transport and an English speaker this far south relieved some of Dylan's anxiety. "Yes, please. How many are waiting?"

"Why wait? I can take you now, alone," the man said. "Come," and he began to walk to a nearby black car without the markings of an official beige taxi. The offer tempted to Dylan as the time neared 4:00. Dylan walked with the man.

"How much?" Dylan asked.

"For you, sir, one hundred."

Dylan reached into his pocket for Lily's instructions and scanned the lines quickly.

TAXI FROM KELAA TO BOUMALNE: 25 MINS = 18 DIRHAMS

He felt the photograph but did not unfold it. The thought of the girls reassured him. The cryptic man offered Dylan no bargain; he could either pay the hundred or wait for more passengers. Peace Corps had given him a carefully-calculated travel allowance that would not cover the eighty-two dirham difference.

"How many are waiting for Boumalne?" Dylan asked.

"Two, plus yourself. The day is short, you may not find enough people and have to stay in Kelaa' tonight. You had better come with me," the man urged.

She said to get to Boumalne by four. She said it's only twenty-five minutes from Kelaa' to Boumalne. I can wait a little longer and see.

"*La shukran*," Dylan said, waving his head and hands to indicate no.

"As you wish," the man said, gently closing the car door.

Dylan walked to the adjacent café and sat down while the man lit a cigarette and stood by the black car. The phone read 3:09 and again Dylan began to sweat.

"*Salamu alaykum*," a man of forty-five with an apron and a tray said dispassionately.

"*Wa alaykum salam*," Dylan replied. "*Nis-nis, afak.*" During training, Dylan had become accustomed to the small drink made of half-instant coffee and half warm milk. The waiter nodded and placed a liter of water on the table with a glass. *Don't touch it, the seal's broken*, he thought. Not wanting to be impolite, Dylan poured some water into the glass to give the appearance that he had sipped some.

Dylan sat back in the chair and watched the cars pass on the busy Kelaa' road. *Almost there. Almost home. Home?* The question intrigued him while he waited for his coffee. *Home was supposed to be with Kayla, but she chose differently. What a nightmare.* He reached in his pocket for his phone and left it on the white plastic table.

The small glass of coffee arrived at 3:16 along with three large lumps of sugar, a tiny spoon, and a shoe-shine boy. *I only wanted coffee.* He wore grey hiking boots made of high-tech fabric, but the undeterred boy set to work with his brush and brown polish.

"*S'il vous plaît, monsieur?*" the boy said as he kneeled. Annoyed, Dylan retracted his feet and unintentionally kicked the quickly moving boy. "*Mah?*" the boy angrily snarled, thrusting his brush toward Dylan.

"*Samhi*," Dylan said deflecting the brush and reaching into his pocket, taking out the remaining coins from the chips he bought at the rest stop and sent the boy on his way. Turning back, the boy extended his hand and asked, "*Avez-vous un stylu, s'il vous plaît?*"

Why do they always ask for fucking pens? He shook his head and the harmless boy disappeared into the vegetable market with his battered shoe-shine box. *What's his story? Is he just looking for pocket change or feeding a family of eight? Someone is always in need here. Is it the same at home and I just don't see it?* Dylan heard a raspy, gurgling voice from across the street.

"Monsieur! Monsieur!"

Dylan looked at the bank and saw no one in the doorway, but looked down at the street and saw a man with a torn t-shirt and a matted, wiry grey beard sitting on the curb.

"Monsieur! Monsieur!" the man repeated, waving a stick—presumably a crutch—in the air. He put his hand to his mouth pleading for food. Dylan froze. *Where did he come from?*

The man had not bathed in some time. He continued to call out to Dylan who just stared back. No one else paid the man on the curb any attention. As Dylan stared, he noticed that the man only had one full, but deformed leg; the other—a stub that looked infected—poked from inside a pair of dirty shorts. His left eye bulged and swelled with a deep red color. While Dylan had encountered similarly pitiful beggars before—even in his first three months in Morocco—he had never before seen someone so obviously needy as this poor soul. *Horror.* Again, to his secular surprise, he silently said a *Hail Mary.*

Dylan's prayer, however, did not appear efficacious; the man still sat and still cried out. Dylan continued to stare despite an intense urge to look away. *Horror.* He repeated the word to himself again and again while continuing to stare at the wretched beggar. *Horror.* Both the word and the pain he felt brought him back to his last encounter with Kayla in November of their senior year. He stood in the kitchen of his apartment, filling a bowl with cereal, wearing only yellow polka-dot boxer shorts—the dotes were white and the shorts were green—and a white shirt that read SPARTANS in green down the long sleeve; the checkered tile felt cool to his bare feet. Kayla stood in the doorway and startled him with her unexpected presence. Through the window over the sink, Dylan saw the yellow-ochre leaves move in the slight breeze.

"*Oh, hey. How was your trip home?*" he had asked.

"*It was ok, I guess.*"

"*Just ok? How are your parents? Did your mom help you with the wedding stuff?*" He had turned his attention back to the cereal.

"*We didn't do any wedding stuff, Dyl.*"

"*Oh. What did you do? Everything ok?*" He had looked up and spilled some milk from the bowl onto the counter. Putting down the half-gallon jug, he had walked toward her, but she retreated slightly into the hallway. She wore snug dark blue jeans and a thin cranberry-colored sweater. *Where's the necklace I gave you for your birthday?* he had wondered. She had pulled back her shoulder-length caramel-colored hair in something of an accidental ponytail. *She always looked great even when she didn't try. I loved holding her waist before kissing her.*

"*Dyl, I, er,*"

"*What Kay, what's up?*"

"*Oh Dyl,*" she had put her face in her hands.

"*Kay, what?*"

"*I don't know how to say it,*" her voice muffled by her hands.

"*What? Tell me,*" he remembered saying as he walked to her, wanting to comfort her.

"*I uh. I had...*"

"*What did you have, Kay?*"

"*I don't know, Dyl.*"

"*Christ, Kayla, just say it. What's up?*"

"I had. An abortion."

"What do you mean, an abortion?"

"An abortion. I was pregnant. I was going..."

"You were pregnant? What?"

"Yeah, I know. I know I should have told you, Dyl. I just didn't. I was scared, I..."

"An abortion?"

"Yes, Dylan. I had an abortion."

"I mean, who?"

"You Dyl, it was only ever you. Please believe me."

"When? I mean, when did it happen?"

"I think it was the morning you proposed, actually. I messed up my pills that week—we had been camping—I thought we'd be fine. I didn't want to say anything, I loved you so much then."

"Wait. You messed up your pills sometime in August and didn't tell me? And then, you find out you're pregnant and you didn't tell me? And then, you have a—an abortion—and you didn't tell me? Kayla, what is this?"

"I'm telling you now, Dyl."

"Now. Are you kidding me? Now?"

"Dyl, I know. I couldn't think straight. I still can't. School. Graduation. Wedding. Law school. It was too much. I just couldn't be pregnant, too."

"Kay. You had an abortion without even telling me you were pregnant. For real? And now I'm supposed to trust you and marry you? How can we make this work in six months? What a horror."

"I know, Dyl. I'm so sorry. You're such a good guy. I'm just so very sorry." As she turned, her crying stopped, and she walked down the dark hallway leaving Dylan standing on the cool linoleum in his polka-dot boxer shorts and Spartans shirt.

34

He clenched his jaw remembering the scene from nearly two years earlier. He had forgotten the rest of the scene, except for the yellow-ochre leaves beyond the window glass. *Horror.* It was the last word he had said to her before she left that day. That moment in the kitchen, as well as the deception leading to it, and the agony that followed had been a horror—for Kayla, the baby, and Dylan. Yes, sadness and pity followed, but Dylan could only ever describe the agony of that moment as horror.

"Monsieur! Monsieur!" The man again called out, drawing Dylan back from his nightmare. Despite his warm face, he felt the coolness of moisture on his cheeks, unsure if from tears or from sweat. Dylan stared again at the man. *Horror. He looks so very horrible.*

Dylan did not shout back, just as he did not shout after Kayla when she stepped into the darkness. Instead, just as he had done after Kayla left, he ran—from the fear, and the pain, and the unknown—a run that took him to that very table in Kelaa' M'Gouna on September 14. Frantically, he opened his wallet to pay for the coffee and pulled out a twenty, which was twice as much as the coffee's worth. In his discomfort and anxiety, he could not stay there any longer and wait for change from the waiter. Looking back across the street, he could still only summon one word: *horror.*

"Monsieur! Monsieur!" the man repeated from across the street, but Dylan chose not to look back—he ran and needed to keep running. The man wailed as Dylan turned with his pack toward the driver and his car. Dylan handed the driver, rather than the man on the curb, a hundred-dirham note. He jumped into the back seat of the car with his pack and hurried the driver. Dylan did not turn to look at the man crying *"Monsieur! Monsieur!"* as the mysterious driver hastened down the road,

presumably toward Boumalne. *Horror.*

Although much more comfortable in the empty car, the drive from Kelaa' to Boumalne passed like it had been from Ouarzazate, with flat sandy stretches surrounded by distant mountains alternating with settlements sliced in two by the paved road. The repetitive landscape failed to interest Dylan this time. *I should have given him money, I should have helped him. I should have given him what was in my pocket*, his thoughts raced while his breathing had become shallow. *Coward. I ran from him. I always run, just like I did from home and the pain there. I avoided the woman on the bus. I can't run anymore; I've got to make this work.* The thoughts haunted him, and while lost in his thoughts, the desert world flashed by.

"Are we close?" he asked. His breathing slowed.

"This is Boumalne, *mon ami.* Where would you like to go?" the driver asked, drawing Dylan back to the present. *I made it. It was harder than I thought, but I made it.*

"I must find Faiz to bring me to Ikniouen. Do you know him?"

"I know Faiz, we all know Faiz. Faiz is a very good man, very good. I will bring you to him and he will bring you to Ikniouen, but Ikniouen is very far from here," the driver told him. Dylan reached into his pocket and again pulled-out the worn piece of folded paper, but did not touch the photograph.

GET TO BOUMALNE BY 4:00 TO MEET FAIZ.

THEN, 2 HOURS TO IKNIOUEN. INSHA'ALLAH

This day will never end. Now I really have to pee.

The driver pulled alongside a line of small street shops and pointed to a white van parked fifty feet ahead. Dylan looked at the phone: 4:06.

"Faiz is there, *mon ami. Bon chance*," the mysterious man said while shifting into park.

"*Shukran*," replied Dylan in thanks as he grabbed his pack and walked toward the van with its door ajar. He found it filled with people and without a driver.

"*Samhi, mani* Faiz?" Dylan asked in Tashelheet without a response from the others.

"Faiz," said a teenage boy, pointing ahead to a middle-aged Moroccan man with a mustache. He wore khaki pants with a faded blue button-down shirt and stood on the sidewalk talking to a shorter, balder man wearing a striped brown sweater and teal-colored pants. Dylan walked to greet them, extending his hand and saying as he had practiced:

"*Salamu alaykum. Isminu Yusuf, sg hay-at salaam*," introducing himself as Yusuf from the Peace Corps. The two men erupted in a chorus of "Yusuf!" They shook hands like they were old friends reunited after many long years. Dylan relaxed. The man in the striped sweater spoke first, in English:

"Yusuf, I welcome you. I am Bouhouch and this is Faiz. We have expected you. Is Yusuf your Christian name? Is it the name of your father?" he asked, holding Dylan's hand.

"My Christian name is Dylan, but I use Yusuf here," he explained, relieved that Bouhouch spoke English so well.

"Yusuf, did you bring salt from Marrakech?" Bouhouch asked, glancing at Faiz.

"Salt?" Dylan asked. *Lily didn't mention salt. Is it rare here? What the hell is he talking about?*

"Yes, salt. You know, in French, *sel*. In Tashelheet we say *tisnt*."

"I do know it, but no…I didn't. I'm sorry…I…er, didn't know," he stuttered and looked down at the cracked cement sidewalk.

Faiz looked at Bouhouch who translated what transpired and the two broke into laughter. Bouhouch shook Dylan's hand even more vigorously now.

"Oh, Yusuf! It is a little joke! We call it *nukta*. We tell people to bring salt to Marrakech in the warm months because you cook there!" Their laughter was contagious.

"*Wa-ha*," Dylan said as he paused and cracked a smile. The laughing continued.

"*Wa-ha. Y'allah, andu*," Faiz announced, ending the handshake and taking the pack from Dylan's back to effortlessly toss it to two boys sitting on the roof.

"Who is that?" one of the roof boys asked in Tashelheet.

"*Usted ujdid*," Faiz replied quietly.

"What did he say, I didn't catch it?" Dylan asked Bouhouch.

"Faiz has said you are the new teacher. That boy is his son. His name is Smail."

Teacher. I like that, even though I'm not really a teacher. Dylan looked up at the boys, smiled, and gave them a thumbs-up, which they returned with giggles.

Bouhouch opened the passenger door and ushered Dylan before he climbed in to share the passenger's seat. After slamming the door, Bouhouch turned to the passengers seated behind and, speaking too quickly for Dylan to follow, said something about "Yusuf" and "*usted*" to which all the passengers applauded. Faiz climbed into the driver's seat and invoked "*bismillah*," to bless the journey.

"*Andu?*" Bouhouch said to Dylan, asking if they would go.

"*Andu*," Dylan repeated with a nod, nervously giving the thumbs-up sign.

"*Y'allah*," Faiz replied resoundingly as he started the engine and drove off.

The next stop, thought Dylan, *will be home. My new home. Without Kayla. It'll be great. It will; although, I wish I had pissed before we left.*

Shortly after they passed through Boumalne, Faiz slowed when he neared a road sign that pointed south and read "IKNIOUEN" in both Roman and Arabic scripts. The van turned slowly so as to not disturb the roof passengers. Looking straight ahead through the windshield, Dylan saw another unfathomable expanse with imposing mountains beyond—*a place for epics*—and only the faintest trace of a dirt road to follow. He felt the phone, the picture, and the folded paper in his pockets. He knew they were there, but he did not need them at that moment—he had met Faiz at nearly four and the great adventure had begun.

"Those are the Saghro Mountains, Yusuf. Ikniouen is in those mountains," Bouhouch said. He turned to Faiz and howled "*Y'allah, andu!*" with a clap.

"*Insha'Allah,*" Faiz laughed and shifted gears as they drove toward the mountain village they all now called home.

Bou Gafr

Dylan heard the donkeys braying. *Always the fucking donkeys*, he thought as he opened his eyes. In the faint early light of that February morning, he flashed on his cheap Nokia phone to see the time: 6:04. *No new messages. Headache. Usually a fucking headache.* Dylan never slept particularly well in that cement apartment: he had a thin mattress on a cold floor and the room felt perpetually damp without any ventilation. He exhaled. *I can see my breath and then it turns to mold on the wall. Who knew Moroccan winters were so miserable?* He set the phone down on the floor next to the dog-eared picture of Kayla with his sister. *Tuesday. School today, for both of you. What a fucking mess it all turned out to be Kayla—I would have been a dad. And now I'm here. Alone. Except for the fucking donkeys.* The braying never stopped on Tuesdays. *Market day*, he said to himself and then repeated it: *market day.*

Coffee first, he thought as he stood, steadied himself, and massaged his temples. To keep the chill out, he pulled grey sweatpants over his purple boxer shorts and then threw his goldenrod *djellaba* over his purple Emerson College t-shirt, preferring to match the shirt with the shorts. As he pulled the heavy robe over his head, his eye noticed the purple t-shirt. *Mackenzie. She'll be center stage soon enough.* Although high school friends, they kept in contact through college, less so when Dylan and Kayla became more serious. They had gone to see her on stage in Boston once and Mackenzie had sent him the shirt as a going-away present. Dylan always remembered part of the note that she enclosed: "*Thank you for pushing me to be my best.*" *She's sweet*, he thought as he fussed with the heavy *djellaba* which, even though he stood more than six feet tall, reached just above his ankles.

Slipping into his well-worn yellow leather Moroccan slippers, he shuffled into the kitchen to brew—no, make—coffee. He had developed something of an addiction to coffee. He disliked the sweetness of both soda and mint tea. College made him an avid coffee drinker and sipping the hot instant drink—always black—from his chipped mug represented a bit of a comfort to him in his new life in the Sahara. *I'm in Africa. The coffee should be great,* he said to himself, *not this Nescafé shit.* The tap gurgled as he turned the faucet, but no water came out. *Fuck,* he said for the third time that morning as he reached for a filled bottle. The tap usually worked, but not always, so he had learned to keep bottles filled. *Still, at least I've got it sometimes, most people here don't,* he reminded himself, taking a deep breath. *Mom said she'd send better coffee, but I can make do with this. It's Peace Corps after all. Mom and Dad did it, so can I.*

He opened the kitchen window and peered out as the kettle heated. The street below thrived on Tuesdays with all manner of people coming and going to *souq*. Both villagers and those from distant desert outposts called *douars* made their way to the weekly market. Men strolled as they carried packages while women—who were rarely seen on the sole street except for on market days—walked in pairs carrying plastic bags with groceries. Children dashed among the crowd enjoying the

41

morning activity of the *souq*. Dylan saw Smail—Faiz's son—and his two friends, boys of about eight, sitting on the stoop opposite his apartment, engrossed in some sort of trade. *It's candy, not dope.* Closer to the market, the insufferable donkeys were tethered to prevent their escape. A camel stood among the donkeys; a rare sight in the village but not out of place with these once nomadic people. The scene appeared harmless—*classic Peace Corps*, he reminded himself. *This is what you came for.*

"*Waaa Usted!*" Smail called to Dylan with a laugh. "Hey, Teacher!"

"*Salamu alaykum*," Dylan replied with a gesture—not even a wave—as the boys laughed. *They're just saying hi, they're harmless. You used to like it. Go back to bed if you want to be an asshole today, ok?* "You three should be in school."

"Not this morning, *Usted*. Today is *souq*," Smail responded in Tashelheet.

"Tomorrow, *insha'Allah*," Dylan said.

"Not tomorrow, it is a holiday," Muhammad—the smallest—yelled back.

What holiday? He wondered about what the boy had said as he latched the window. Dylan turned and looked in the kitchen, now darker with the opaque window closed. A counter ran along one wall and a small white plastic table and two chairs along with the other, filling the small space. His aluminum *tagine*, a plastic crate, and a pile of dishes sat on the counter made of mismatched pastel tiles. In the crate rested four shriveled carrots, two onions, and a very tired potato.

"*Arba hisu, sin azalim, yan battata*," he said aloud, practicing his *souq* vocabulary. *It's not the shopping, I'm good with my numbers*, he reasoned. *Well, pretty good, except when I asked for a quarter kilo of cheese and got four. Ha,* the memory made

42

him laugh. *It's the conversation. I suck at it. I can only ask 'How is your family?' so many times.* Speaking Tashelheet frustrated Dylan. He excelled in many things, but not languages. For seventeen months he had survived in the village giving competent, although shallow, health lessons at the school. *I need to interact more with them*, he encouraged himself, turning his attention back to his kettle. *I came here to do this.*

He took off the *djellaba*, sweatpants, and t-shirt. *It's fucking colder here than in Williamstown.* He put on new clothes: navy boxer shorts, jeans, and a few layers of shirts—a white under-shirt, an old long-sleeve cotton shirt from his high school that read SPARTANS down the sleeve, and then a navy-blue t-shirt on top. The cuffs of the long-sleeved shirt frayed years ago, but he kept sentimental things. The navy-blue t-shirt had been a gift from another friend, this one at American University. He looked down and ran his fingers over the red and white letters. *Emma. Home.* He sighed. *Knock it off, you've got shit to do today,* he said aloud as he continued dressing. Layering shirts, he had learned, suited him best in the mountains, which varied between a malevolent sun and chilling shadows. Rather than comb his light brown tousled hair, he simply put on his Williams ball cap and braced himself for the street below. He stuffed the sealed letter he had written to his sister Aly into his back pocket. The inconsequential letter summarized the few things he had done that week; he liked to describe what he saw in the desert.

"*Bonjour!*" the boys said in unison as Dylan opened the door and stepped into the sunlight.

"*Salamu alaykum*" Dylan returned with a grimace. *I'm Amer-ican*, he thought, *not French. They should know after more than a year. Why do they tease me?* Forcing a smile, he waved and locked the door. *Don't be an asshole today. For real.*

"*Mani tudut, Usted?*" Smail asked him where he was going.

"*L'busta,*" Dylan said, showing them the letter from his back pocket.

"For your wife?" Smail burst into laughter as he questioned Dylan in Tashelheet.

"My sister. I have no wife. Women are too difficult, Smail."

"We know," little Mohammad said, reigniting the laughter.

"Ha," Dylan said at the retort betraying a smile as he set off toward the market.

For six days each week, the *souq* remained an empty, dusty square, but on Tuesdays it came alive with tents and men selling everything from shoes to sheep.

"*Salaam, salaam,*" Dylan casually greeted passersby as he walked up the dirt street.

"*Wa alaykum salam,*" he repeatedly heard in return as he continued on his way. The men in the street watched him intently, but they returned to their business as he walked. *What do they stare at?* He bypassed the *souq*, again turning left, and headed toward the post office situated only a few more yards beyond. He might have avoided the busy post office on market days, but Dylan liked the routine of checking his mailbox every morning and seeing the kindly postmaster who forgave his tortured Tashelheet. Before turning right at the only lamppost in the village, which bore a small *Poste Maroc* sign, he saw two men on ladders ahead. They struggled to hang red bunting—Moroccan flags—on the walls of the municipal office building. *Holiday*, he remembered. Stepping into the dim cement building, he found a market-day bundle—not a line—of men at the counter. Abdullah, the postmaster, looked up and greeted Dylan using his rudimentary English.

44

"Good mornings, Mister Yusuf," he said while nodding. The entire group of men turned their attention from the counter to Dylan in the open doorway. The men stood uniformly shorter than Dylan. All of them needed a shave, and most wore knit caps and dark-colored *djellabas*, although Abdullah wore an old white shirt with an Oxford collar. The unheated cement lobby felt cold like Dylan's apartment.

"*Salamu alaykum*, Sidi Abdullah," Dylan responded as he walked to the wall of post office boxes and inserted his key into the lock of number fourteen.

"You have no mails today, Yusuf," Abdullah told him before he could turn the key. Dylan nodded, acknowledging his disappointment with a grimace.

"*Shukran*," Dylan responded. He reached into his back pocket, pulled out the letter for his sister, and stood at the rear of the group. The postmaster reached across the counter indicating to the other men to move aside, extending his hand toward Dylan.

"*Samhi, samhi,*" Dylan excused himself as he walked toward the counter. The men grunted and Dylan heard some *"ya, yas"* but they, too, like the men in the street, seemed to pay him little attention. Dylan blushed, he disliked special treatment in the village; he already felt different enough. The men crowded around Dylan as he handed Abdullah the letter over the counter.

"*Sa Merica, afak,*" Dylan indicated the letter's destination.

The gathered whispered and nodded among themselves, *"Merica, Merica."* Abdullah studied the letter carefully, intrigued by Dylan's handwriting. He reached into his drawer and found an airmail stamp—bearing the portrait of the young king Muhammad—and affixed it, then forcefully cancelled it. Abdullah appeared to derive some satisfaction in pounding the letter, and the king's portrait, with such vigor.

45

"Mumtaz," Dylan said with approval, giving Abdullah a thumbs-up. The men copied him and one even patted Dylan on the back, repeating *"mumtaz"* aloud. Dylan pulled some dirham notes from his wallet to pay for the stamp while Abdullah continued to study the envelope with his mechanical Roman script. "Here it says Dy-lan, but you say Yusuf, why?" Abdullah inquired as he had many times before.

"There is no Tashelheet name for Dylan. I like Yusuf, it is Muslim and Christian."

"Yes, Jo-seph," Abdullah said slowly. "Here, you write A-lee," pointing to Aly's address. "She is your sister."

"Yes, my sister. In Massachusetts," Dylan anticipated Abdullah's next question.

"I cannot say it," Abdullah said shaking his head. They both laughed as Abdullah deposited the letter in a large burlap bag on the counter.

"Shukran bezzef!" Dylan said. "Sidi Abdullah, why do the men put flags at the Commune? Is it a holiday?"

"Tomorrow is the Bou Gafr festival. Seventy-five years since the war. It is good," Abdullah replied. "Your family is well? Your sister and your father and your mother?"

"Kulshi labas, l'hamdullah," Dylan confirmed.

"L'hamdulillah," Abdullah replied, seeming genuinely grateful to God for their health by customarily folding his hands over his heart. Staring at Dylan's shirt, he parsed, "A-mer-i-can U-ni-ver-si-ty. It is your school?"

"No, my friend. Her name is Em-ma."

"Your friend. It is a girl?"

"Yes, she is a woman. In America, men and women are sometimes friends."

"It is good. We are friends, Yusuf, here in al-Maghreb."

46

"*Shukran*, Sidi Abdullah," Dylan said, also folding his hands over his heart. The sentiment was lost when a man reached over Dylan's shoulder and handed Abdullah twenty dirhams. "No post tomorrow, then?"

"No post, Sidi Yusuf. Holiday," he said, returning to his work.

Dylan stepped out into the bright sunlight. *Abdullah is kind.*

Even at home in Massachusetts, Dylan preferred convenience shopping rather than bargain hunting. As he approached the market from the post office, he headed for the tent closest to the street rather than shop for the best price among the four or five grocers.

"*Salamu alaykum,*" he greeted the men sitting on the ground under the canvas tarp.

"*Wa alaykum salam*, Yusuf. *Labas?* What would you like?" the man asked in Tashelheet.

Regardless of what remained in his kitchen, Dylan kept his order the same every week: two kilograms each of tomatoes, potatoes, and carrots with a couple of extra onions. In September he bought pomegranates and in the summer melons, but in winter he enjoyed little diversity in his diet. He really only needed to buy vegetables at the weekly market; Brahim sold the rest of his staples—couscous, cheese, yogurt, milk, and chicken—at the small village *hanoot*. On market days, the line for Brahim's shop extended far into the street. *I'll go tomorrow,* he always thought when he saw the line.

"I'd like a fat one, please," Dylan said, pointing to the crate of onions.

The man looked puzzled.

"*Azalim?*" the man asked.

"Yeah, a fat onion," Dylan said in Tashelheet, frustrated by his inarticulateness.

The seller proceeded to count nine onions.

"Not nine. A fat one! Forget it. *Joojz azalim. Safi*," Dylan said with impatience, explaining that two were enough and realizing the sloppiness of his pronunciation.

"*Wa-ha, joojz. Mashi mushkil*, Yusuf," the seller said, reassuring Dylan it was no problem. "And an extra potato for luck. This potato is very lucky, Yusuf," he said cryptically in Tashelheet while laughing. "You need luck because you have no wife!"

What does he mean, lucky? Who gives a potato for luck? They are so fucking weird.

The seller put the ordinary potato with the other vegetables into black plastic bags for Dylan to carry, and they exchanged money, thanks, as well as handshakes. The man continued to quietly chuckle as he explained what had happened to the neighboring seller. *"He thought he said fat,"* Dylan overheard the seller say while turning back toward the street.

Dylan eyed the date-sellers as he left the market square. He liked dates, but these were always a sticky mess piled high on a dirty table that attracted legions of flies. Every week he passed them feeling nauseous. *Nasty.* Focused on the dates, Dylan rounded the corner and entered the busy street carrying his plastic bags of vegetables. Dodging a pile of goat shit in the road, he unexpectedly stood face to face with the camel he had seen from the kitchen window. He retreated from the grunting giant with black eyes. The size and smell of the camel amazed, and perhaps even scared, him. *Fuck*, he said not-so-quietly and heard laughter behind him.

"Yusuf!" someone shouted. "Yusuf!" Bouhouch waved as he approached.

"*Salamu alaykum*, Yusuf." Bouhouch greeted Dylan with a

typically long handshake. "*Labas?* How is your father? And your mother? And your sister? And You? You are well?" Bouhouch repeated the greeting in both Berber and Arabic. "You have health?"

"I do, *l'hamdullah.*" Dylan responded in English, emphasizing, "Thanks be to God."

"Thanks be to God," confirmed Bouhouch. Dylan had learned—well into his year of service—that Hussein was his first name, but he preferred his surname of Bouhouch. He was short, fortyish, with a mustache and slight growth of beard. Usually, he wore a striped knit sweater—tan and brown—with teal colored pants, except for Friday, when, like all the other men, he wore a white *djellaba* for mosque prayers. Dylan often wondered what Bouhouch did for a living because he never traveled far from the village and, thankfully, spoke fluent English. Lily, the previous volunteer in the village had been right. Bouhouch served as the local godfather. "What are you doing, Yusuf?"

"I went to the post office and then I bought my vegetables," he said, lifting the plastic bags he carried. "I must buy bread from your brother."

"*Mezyan*, Yusuf. Very good. Every day you must buy bread because you have no wife! Poor you!" he admonished while releasing his grip and resting his hand on Dylan's shoulder. The slight rebuke served as an often-used line among the village men—and even the boys like Smail—who seemed to genuinely pity Dylan's bachelorhood.

"In America, we don't marry at my age." The deception made Dylan blush considering he and Kayla had been engaged two years earlier.

"Faiz had two wives at your age, Yusuf. But it is ok. You are poor. You are Peace Corps. We will find you a good Tamazight girl to marry." He patted Dylan's shoulder as he started to laugh, still pronouncing the "s" in Corps.

They always try to get me married. Again he thought of Kayla and his bags of vegetables felt heavy, so he set them down on the dirt road.

"Yusuf, what will you do tomorrow?" Bouhouch asked.

"Tomorrow I will teach," Dylan explained his work in Ikniouen as teaching. The description was slightly inaccurate because he was not a teacher for the Ministry of Education, despite that people called him "usted." He only sporadically assisted at the middle school. Although he helped with multiple village projects, he kept a flexible schedule. He also did not understand the Moroccan calendar and had several times before arrived at the school to find it closed.

"Yusuf, tomorrow is a holiday and you will not teach. We will go to Bou Gafr; you must join us. You know the story of Bou Gafr?"

"Yes. *Hajj* tells the story often when the tribe fought the French at the mountain. I think it during the winter of 1932. I have wanted to go since I first heard the story."

"1933, Yusuf. It is, how do you say—epics. Like your American Valley Forge, no?"

"Epic. And yes, Valley Forge was also difficult for George Washington."

"Our hero is the leader Assu u-ba Slam and the school is named for him. You must join us tomorrow, Yusuf."

"Yes, I would like to go," he replied. "But why are you going? Isn't Bou Gafr far?"

"It is not far. We will go to remember the seventy-five years. What do you call it?"

"An anniversary?" asked Dylan, after thinking for a moment. Bouhouch had studied English at university but occasionally relied on Dylan to fill in the gaps of his knowledge.

"Yes, an anniversary. Like in French. My English is poor but better than your Tashelheet, Yusuf! Every day you must practice your Tashelheet, it is very, very important. How will you talk to your Tamazight wife when you are married?"

"*Wa-ha*," Dylan said unenthusiastically, knowing the rebuke was harmless.

"*Mezyan.* We will go at eight."

"New eight or old eight?" Dylan asked. Since Morocco had, for the first time, adopted Daylight Savings Time that year, confusion had emerged in the village as to how to measure time during the winter months.

"Yusuf! Come at eight-thirty. Maybe you will be early or maybe you late!" Bouhouch laughed patting Dylan's shoulder. "It is Moroccan time, Yusuf. *Mashi mushkil!*"

"*Wa-ha.* Yeah, I know. How long will we be gone?"

"Only the morning; we will eat kebabs and return. Brahim and others will come."

"How will we go?"

"Faiz will drive us and then we will walk. I do not think it is far, I have not been."

"You have never been? Has Faiz?" Dylan asked.

"No, but we will bring *Hajj*, he will know. It is no problem, Yusuf. *Mashi mushkil!*"

Everything here is 'mashi mushkil,' they never have problems, Dylan thought.

"*Ar aska*, Yusuf?" Bouhouch asked as he confirmed the plans for Wednesday.

"Until then, *insha'Allah*," Dylan responded with a handshake.

He had grown accustomed to using *insha'Allah*, which means "God willing," when talking about the future.

"*Insha'Allah*," Bouhouch returned. Dylan lifted his grocery bags and turned into the bakery while Bouhouch disappeared into the crowded *souq*.

Market days filled only the morning. In the afternoon, some men went to the mosque for prayers while others gathered with family and friends for a meal. Some of the children went to school. Since the market drew the villagers and also those of the *douars* into Ikniouen, the day provided a good social opportunity to meet with old friends. Dylan often received lunch invitations and enjoyed the ritual of eating. He never fussed about what he ate provided it did not look like offal, he had good manners, and despite his limited use of Tashelheet, could make appropriate dinner conversation. This Tuesday, however, he had not received an invitation to dinner and it suited him just fine. He boiled water for more coffee, ate some bread and packaged cheese, more likely plastic than cheese, and sat in the warmth of the sunlight that streamed in through the glass of the kitchen window.

His thick paperback copy of The Pickwick Papers lay on the white plastic kitchen table. The folded paper from his first journey to Ikniouen more than a year earlier—another memento of his travels—marked his page. The bit of exposed paper caught his eye and he remembered that harried day traveling from Marrakech to the mountain village. *It worked out, I've made it more than a year.* One quiet Sunday after he had settled in his apartment, he scratched some names and words at the top of the paper. They were birthdays he probably wouldn't forget—except for his friend John's, which he never could remember—but writing the dates had eased his homesickness that Sunday. He had found some astrology references on the backside of some newspaper his mother had sent him and he played with the words.

Kayla—Oct 19. Libra...smart + diplomatic. Really? ~~Yes NO~~ *yes*
Aly—May 13. Total Taurus...bull-headed, hates change. 100% sis.
John—Sept 22(?) Virgo? Paper says like Mother Teresa. Joke?
Mackenzie—July 28. Leo, not a lion, but loves *the limelight. True*
Christine—Dec. 12. Sagittarius. The archer. Aim's high. Always.

He stared at Kayla's name peeking out from the pages of the book. *She hadn't been any of those things that day in the kitchen. Hiding a pregnancy and then having an abortion—hardly smart, hardly diplomatic, hardly a peacemaker.* He looked at the other names. *Aly is the sweetest bull I've ever known, though I'm sure she's tougher with her friends than me. I wonder how John likes California? I've not heard from him since the t-shirt arrived in the mail. Both Kenzie and Christine are just great, whenever I hear from them. Home.* A donkey brayed outside. *Fucking donkeys. Abdullah and Bouhouch are nice, but they're not friends. Sometimes I feel welcomed, sometimes I feel so alone.* His eyes moved back up the list to Kayla. *Move on, Dyl. For God's sake, move on. You came here to move on.* He opened the marked page and inserted the paper deeper into the book, hiding it from view.

"*Waaa Usted,*" the street boys' shout again broke his thoughts but this time made him smile. *Harmless.* Dylan opened the window, waved, and the three boys giggled as they scrambled up the road toward the market. *Teacher,* he thought as he smiled and reached to close the window.

Wednesday morning began much quieter than the previous market day and Dylan roused himself a little after seven. *Headache again. No fucking donkeys on Wednesday, though,* he said after he yawned as he wiped the sleep from his eyes. *Perfect.* He glanced at the picture of Kayla and Aly but put his head back on the thin pillow and closed his eyes. *Big day. It's ok, I got this.* The need to pee, however, forced him out of the small bedroom more than his feelings about the day ahead.

The unheated air felt too cold on his stomach to wash in, so he threw on his jeans and several layers for warmth, including the grey Belmont University t-shirt John had sent him. The accompanying note had only read: *"Watch out for snakes, Indiana, and don't be an asp out there." Clever. Always clever.* After he mechanically made his instant coffee, he opened the kitchen window while he sipped from the chipped mug. *So quiet today.* Before lacing-up his hiking boots, he grabbed his old leather knapsack and added two liters of water, not bothering to take any other supplies. *Bouhouch said it wasn't far.* He looked at his phone with disappointment: again, no new messages. He rarely received text messages from other volunteers but welcomed the few he did. *It's my fault, I didn't make many friends during training.* On Sundays, his parents and sister often called—and he enjoyed that. He had called Kayla just twice in his first year away. The first time, on her birthday, she did not answer. *Weird overseas phone number on her caller id*, he reassured himself before leaving a message:

"Hey, Kay. Happy birthday. Things are pretty good, er, great here. Hope you're okay. Really."

At Christmas, however, she answered after just two rings.

"Hey Dyl. Merry Christmas."

"Hey Kay, same to you. I'm so glad you picked up."

"It mustn't be Christmas there, huh?"

"Nope. Just another day. Me and the camels. Are you good? We

haven't talked since I left, and even then, it was, well, you know, weird. I guess I worried I'd die out here, but that's hardly the case."

"Yeah. School and work keep me busy. Wish I could just focus on school but got to pay for it. How's Aly? It's her senior year, right?"

"She's good, almost graduated. Just another semester. It's really good to hear your voice, Kay."

"Thanks, Dyl. Stay safe out there, ok? I've got to go. Family stuff. Jay's telling jokes and Mom's getting mad. Do you remember? Yeah, you probably do remember. Merry Christmas, Dyl."

"You, too, Kay. Let's talk soon."

"Bye Dyl."

The memory, like the phone call, and like so many things between them, had come to an end. He decided not to call the next Christmas. He placed the phone and its sense of security on the kitchen table. *Why bring it? There's no connection in the desert where I'm going.*

Bouhouch stood in the middle of the road near his brother's bakery, where he and Dylan parted the previous day. He counted members of the group like students: "*yan, sin, shrad...*" Ten had assembled: Bouhouch, his friends, Brahim the handyman-shopkeeper, and an elderly *hajj* wearing a blue *djellaba* and white turban. Faiz, their driver, numbered eleven. Dylan joined the group, shaking hands and exchanging the customary greetings. Everyone was well. Everyone's family was well. Everyone's mother and father were well. Thanks be to God.

"Yusuf, you have bread?" Bouhouch asked, pointing at Dylan.

"*La,*" Dylan said. *Why did I need to bring bread? His brother is the baker.*

"Yusuf!" exclaimed Bouhouch, "We must have bread to eat!" He turned to the rest of the group and spoke in Tashelheet, relating the story to them. Dylan counted the word for bread—*"agrum"*—five times in the story. *Bouhouch knows how to deliver a line—every time.* The men laughed and Dylan blushed a little in his embarrassment.

Dylan easily fixed the problem; he walked to the baker, bought a few round loaves for a dirham each, and rejoined the group. When he returned, Bouhouch nodded to Dylan.

"Andu?" Bouhouch asked.

"Andu," Dylan returned.

"Y'allah," Bouhouch shouted and they all climbed into Faiz's old white van.

"Bismillah!" cried the *hajj* in blue, invoking divine favor on the journey as Faiz rolled the door shut and darkening the cabin. *No turning back now, I guess.* Dylan faced forward to look out through the cracked windshield.

"Andu?" Faiz asked Dylan if they should go while climbing into the driver's seat.

"Andu," he again confirmed with an apprehensive crack in his voice. A chorus of *"andus"* resonated in the van. *Are they mocking me or just curious when they repeat? I never know.*

"Ihallah. Ihallah," Faiz reassured with a nod, encouraging Dylan that it would be good before he cranked the ignition of the ancient machine.

"Ihallah," the *hajj* parroted, slapping Dylan on the shoulder from behind. *"Ihallah."*

Dylan still stared forward. *Relax, he's right, it's good. This is what Dad called the great adventure. Go with it.* He turned and nodded at the *hajj*, but said nothing.

The van rolled toward the edge of town, navigating between the two boulders that stood as sentinels for the village. Children ran from the fields to greet the machine as it tottered over the rough dirt road. As the terrain flattened and the road widened, Faiz gained speed and the children could not maintain the pace. He drove beyond the little arable land in the area, a patch of earth fed by a noisy gas-powered well and worked by several families. Farmers rested against their rakes to watch the van pass by, never raising an arm to wave.

Inside, the stuffy van lacked seats and passenger windows. Dylan and the others arranged themselves on the rock-hard sacks of grain that lined the floor. Beginning their climb higher into the mountains, Faiz shifted gears, the engine groaned, and the *hajj* began to sing a song with a thunderous clap. The sound was pleasant at first but repetitive to Dylan's untutored ear. The gang of eleven happily sang and clapped as they lumbered along the rocky path higher into the mountains while Dylan inattentively watched.

"*Meskeen* Yusuf!" the old *hajj* said, meaning "poor Yusuf." Dylan nodded, knowing the sentiment rang somewhat true; despite being surrounded by the other men in the van, he again noticed loneliness as he played with the hem of his grey t-shirt.

"*Andu?*" the old man repeated to himself as he took a small plastic bag from his *djellaba*. Pulling the bag close to his old eyes to see it, and untying the knot, he opened the plastic and offered a date to Dylan, who obeyed the laws of desert hospitality and accepted it with a "*shukran*." The date came from the fly-covered table at the market; it tasted stale, fibrous, and too sweet. Dylan graciously chewed and swallowed it, a bit remorseful that he had accepted it in the first place. He put its stone in his pocket and continued to look out of the cracked windshield at the expanse of land that lay ahead. Removing his hat, Dylan massaged his temples. *Still hurts a little, and the singing and the bumps aren't helping.*

When the seemingly unending song finished, Bouhouch turned to Dylan and asked: "Yusuf, you know of our hero, Assu u-Ba Slam?"

"You mentioned him yesterday—the tribe's hero, like George Washington."

"Yes, like George Washington; the greatest man our people have ever known," Bouhouch said, extending three fingers. "Assu u-Ba Slam brought our people to this wilderness for three reasons. He believed the French would find three enemies in these mountains: *asimmid*, *izran*, and *nhas*." Although Bouhouch spoke mostly in English to Dylan, the other men overheard the Tashelheet words. They nodded approvingly and repeated them to each other. Dylan knew that *asimmid* means cold and *izran* means rocks. *Yeah, it's cold and rocky, that would suck for the French.*

"*Nhas?*" Dylan asked.

"Copper. Bullets. The third enemy of the French," he said as he extended his arms to represent a rifle. The men in the van nodded and repeated "*ya, ya. Nhas,*" before Bouhouch turned to start another conversation with the men.

The van crawled along, growling under the strain of its load and the difficulty of its terrain, winding through the nothingness for nearly an hour. Staring out of the smudged windshield, Dylan understood how the stony landscape had hardened the tribe. Their ancestors who had fought the French in that desert, which they called the wasteland, had proved that they could withstand cold, rocks, and bullets. Dylan respected their fortitude and strength, but he also found himself missing the leafy trees and grassy hills of home. The men continued to chat, but Dylan quietly looked at the seeming badlands that surrounded him. *It's lonely here,* he thought amidst the chatter.

Increasingly, he became aware of the smells of the van, first its exhaust and then the odors of the bodies. He also thought he smelled goat, although he saw none in the van. He tried to breathe more shallowly, but it proved futile, and the scents continued to upset his stomach. The lonely date sat heavy, its sweetness adding to his nausea. Sounds echoed in his head: the roar of the van, the talk of the men, and the ululation of a woman now coming from Faiz's cassette deck. Dylan could see very little as they climbed higher and higher, with only the road in front of him. He feared, given the steepness of the incline, that they might fall over backward. *Chill. Faiz always knows where he's going. Trust him.*

He glanced down and saw the grey of his Belmont t-shirt exposed from beneath his orange pullover. He felt the trim between his fingers, remembering first John, but then, as so often happened, turned his thoughts to his time at Williams. *College was great: books, ideas, road trips, hikes, Kayla, sex. This isn't great.* He continued to feel the soft cotton as he looked ahead. *What have I done this year? Some toothbrushing and handwashing lessons. I've barely learned the language and I don't feel like I've made any friends, not with other volunteers and not with villagers. And I still miss Kayla. Even though I'm still pissed at her most of the time. I wish, oh Christ how I wish things had been so fucking different. Hor—*

Faiz steered into a pothole, jarring the passengers and forcing Dylan to brace himself amidst shouts of *"ya, ya, ya."*

"*Ishka,*" the *hajj* said shaking his head and explaining that the road was difficult. Dylan nodded in agreement while trying to cling to his meandering memories.

Lily said to make friends. Am I? Aly says to get over Kayla. Am I? Mom and Dad always say to do good work. Am I? Is a mountain hike really what I came here to do?

Without warning or landmark, Faiz stopped the van and they alighted. Dylan looked south; the warmth of the sun on his face felt nice in contrast to the crisp air. Before them rose an unimpressive knoll. In the distance, some peaks stood taller, but these lacked the same scale as those found throughout the rest of the Saghro range.

"*Mani* Bou Gafr?" Dylan inquired about the battle site and confusion ensued among the group. None of the men appeared sure which mountain they had come to climb.

"Bou Gafr," said the old *hajj* solemnly, pointing to the knoll before them.

Is this a fucking joke? I'll eat back at home and skip the kebabs.

They gathered their things and set out. Some, like Dylan, carried plastic bottles of water while others did not. Brahim had a stuffed knapsack; as the village shopkeeper and handyman, he kept a collection of useful items with him. Dylan lifted his own knapsack but slouched his shoulders, slightly disappointed. *This is hardly Valley Forge. I got this.*

The band made for the south with the *hajj* setting a brisk pace.

"How old is the *hajj that he can walk so quickly?*" Dylan breathlessly asked Bouhouch.

"I don't know, I will ask," Bouhouch said and turned to ask the group in Tashelheet. There were many responses from the men. Dylan heard one say "seventy" and another say "ninety-four," but the old *hajj* himself did not answer. He either stood out of earshot or simply ignored the question.

"They say he is in his eighties, but you know, we Ait 'Atta don't count birthdays. He was a boy at the battle." Dylan nodded his head in understanding.

The old man's speed and energy doubled Dylan's as they

started across the rocky desert toward the hill. At twenty-three, Dylan kept himself in decent shape, but no one would consider him athletic. *Kayla always wanted me to run with her, but it bored me. The hajj runs like a kid goat, even in his djellaba.* Occasionally, the old man stopped and looked across the great cavern before them shouting "yo-ho, yo-ho," letting his voice carry to any lonely shepherd who might hear it in that otherwise empty space. His dark and heavily wrinkled face revealed only four teeth when he smiled. His simple blue *djellaba* clearly kept him warm for many years.

He's like my grandfather—he was a runner, a marathoner, even. I miss home, but he'd be proud of me here. Dylan smiled. *They are good people here. Like my family back home.* At the hillcrest, an unending panorama of mountains and gorges—masked at the start—unfolded to the south that had been obscured from the starting point. *Assu u-ba Slam hid here for sure.*

"Bou Gafr?" Dylan asked as he drank heartily from his water bottle. The air felt dry and cool, perhaps only seventy, but they had moved quickly and Dylan perspired. Again the old man shook his head, and the other men pointed to surrounding peaks much fiercer in form than the initial hill had been. But rather than laugh at Dylan, the old *hajj* pointed across the valley to a frightening three-peaked summit, and said only, "Bou Gafr."

The landscape now terrified Dylan. They would have to descend into the gorge to the base of the mountain before ascending to the summit. *Epic,* he thought. *In every fucking way.* Dylan had no idea how tall the mountain stood, and they had already climbed considerably since leaving the village.

"Bouhouch, how long to get there?" Dylan asked between sips of water. The level in his bottle had diminished quickly. *I've got to make this last,* he thought, looking at the bottle.

61

"Who knows Yusuf; when do Berbers wear the watches? *Y'allah!*" He repeated the line in Tashelheet and pointed to his wrist; the others laughed as they resumed their trek.

Within minutes, the *hajj* had again run ahead and vanished.

"Why does he run ahead?" Dylan asked Bouhouch, walking at the rear of the pack.

"His spirit, Yusuf, is in these mountains. Here, he is free."

"Oh," Dylan said skeptically. *I wish he'd stay with us. This is nowhere—if something happens to me, nobody's going to find me. Ever.* His dry mouth prevented him from swallowing.

For the next hour, they descended rather than climbed. A trickle of a river split the thirsty earth at the bottom of the gorge and the water looked cool and inviting to Dylan. While the earlier view from above suggested they would traverse a small sierra to reach Bou Gafr, the riverbed they followed wound around these sharp-faced peaks.

Bouhouch talked with his friends while Dylan turned his attention inward. *She'd love the climbing here, but she'd hate everything else. How many summer days did we climb at home? So great. She was better at it—she was the athlete, I was the thinker everyone said. We were a good match; similar and different,* he thought as he quickened his pace. *It was fucking great—this isn't.*

Dylan's introspection was interrupted as the men gathered around an abandoned stone well. The men lowered a rope and bucket into the dark hole and then drank.

"Who dug the well, Bouhouch?"

"Who? The people, Yusuf."

"What people?" Dylan pushed.

"The mountains people. They are good people. Very good *Amazighen* people. Very strong. They are free. Come, you must drink."

"Where are they now?" Dylan continued to ask.

"Some, very few, still live in the mountains. The rest are gone. Drink the water."

"Thank you, but no. I have my bottles." *I can't believe I didn't bring the iodine. Idiot.*

"As you wish, Yusuf. As you wish."

"Drink Yusuf," urged Brahim in Tashelheet, "this is the only water we will pass."

"*Ihallah.* I have water. *Ihallah,*" Dylan returned. He tortured the phrase with his elementary knowledge of Tashelheet. He meant to reassure Brahim and say that his own water was "good" but he could not construct the phrase in his mind. He dared not drink the untreated well water even though he still had the ascent and return. *That's bacteria in a bucket.*

"*Ihallah,*" Dylan repeated as he cautiously examined the purified water in his plastic bottle and refused the well water. Bouhouch spoke to Brahim in Tashelheet faster than Dylan could comprehend and then turned to Dylan.

"You are well, Yusuf?"

"I am," said Dylan with a smile.

"Then we go. *Y'allah!*" yelled Bouhouch and again they set out for Bou Gafr.

Dylan continued to think as they walked. *Dad called this the great adventure. But I didn't plan this as an adventure, I fell into this because I didn't have any plans or any plans without Kayla. Our life together was going to be great. And now, I'm sort of lost. Lost in the desert. With no water. Even though I came here to find myself.*

After another hour of walking, the group reassembled at an open plateau where a cement monolith covered in graffiti of Amazigh symbols stood at the base of what was clearly Bou Gafr. Dylan touched the solitary marker that bore no plaque—the observer had to recall what transpired there seventy-five years earlier. *No cemetery for their war dead, the mountain is their gravestone.* In the distance, a small stone house with a corrugated roof stood as the lone sentry over the scene—without any sign of its inhabitants. *How'd they carry the metal roof out here?* he asked himself. The group appeared to be alone in the silent wilderness. He felt the weight of the remaining water in his knapsack. *Save it, you're ok.*

"*Yusuf labas?*" Brahim asked.

"*Labas, l'hamdullah,*" Dylan replied, genuinely thanking God. As he reached into his knapsack for his water bottle, he remembered the loaves. His stomach growled as he felt the bread. *Wait for the summit.*

"*Ihallah,*" the hajj interjected, reminding all the day was good.

"*Ihallah,*" Dylan repeated confidently. "*Ihallah.*"

"*Y'allah,*" yelled Bouhouch, this time as a battle cry, and they began their ascent. Much of the climb lacked a discernible path and the men found only a sheer graveled face to negotiate. Despite his fatigue and thirst, Dylan now kept pace with the others, seeming to become like them in their final advance. His feet were sweating and he knew they were blistering as he took each step upwards in his expensive boots, but he continued onward. He glanced at Bouhouch's shoes: brown dress shoes made of faux leather that surely cut into his feet. If Bouhouch—or anyone else—felt pain, he made no sign. The tribesmen and Dylan appeared different—in dress, creed, and language—and yet they shared a common goal that day: to hike, yes; but more importantly, to remember the fallen. The spirit of the great hero Assu u-ba Slam surely walked with them all, and Dylan, too.

As they climbed, keen eyes spotted pieces of shrapnel among

the gravel, rusted memories of the campaign they commemo-
rated. At the summit, Dylan bent over to catch his breath. He
removed layers of his shirts to let his body breathe while the
other men looked at the stone expanse before them. This was
the wasteland they had all come to remember. Rather than look
out in the distance, however, the old *hajj* peered over the edge of
the mountaintop and looked down. "What does he see?" Dylan
asked Bouhouch.

"*Waaa hajj!*" Bouhouch yelled to get the old man's attention
while walking toward him. The two conversed for a minute
before Bouhouch returned the few steps to Dylan.

"He says when the French surrounded the mountain and
trapped our people, every night a woman climbed down the
mountain from there to go to the well. He says that the French
admired her courage so much that no one fired at her. Each
night she climbed down to get water, and each night the French
watched her, for a month's time."

"How many died?" asked Dylan, conscious of the scarcity of
water in that place.

"Thousands. Only five hundred surrendered with Assu u-Ba
Slam. These things we remember, Yusuf." Bouhouch returned
to the *hajj* and they stared silently at the wasteland.

Dylan perched himself on a boulder to contemplate the scene.
He thought about Bouhouch's story. *The numbers don't add
up. One woman climbing down a mountain couldn't bring enough
water to keep thousands hydrated each night. Stories*, he thought.
Berber stories. Are they any different than those of Virgil or Dante?

Brahim made a small fire, amazing Dylan by how he sustained
it with bits of scrounged twigs and the scrub brush called *l-fsa*.
With the fire burning, Brahim boiled water for tea taken from
a bottle. He pulled much of a skinned goat carcass from his

knapsack and cut kebabs to roast and share. *Why not walk the goat up the mountain and then kill it, rather than carry it?* Dylan asked himself as he added the loaves of bread he had carried. The cold winter air refreshed the nose and cheeks, but the sun provided just enough warmth to prevent a chill. Dylan only wore a thin white undershirt as he still felt warm from the climb. He unlaced his boots to allow his feet to dry and stared into the distance, too tired to do anything else.

The sight appeared as unlike anything he knew and the emptiness before him made his thoughts poetic. In its barrenness, the desert was lonely; in its harshness, the desert was fierce. The wilderness had demanded his strength and endurance and it now commanded his respect and fortitude. *It's almost scary here. I wonder what it sounded like when the earth broke apart and pushed these stones toward heaven?* Yet, the desert that day was also mystical and inviting: this was the desert of the spirit: the desert of Moses and Muhammad, of Jesus and John the Baptist, where the holy man encountered the divine and endured the tests put before him. This was the desert of isolation, of long-lost warriors who fled to nowhere in order to find something. The men he accompanied that day were the descendants of those who not only endured the wasteland but also conquered it. Staring at this true wilderness, Dylan slightly and unnoticeably bowed his head in awe.

"Yusuf is always thinking. Come, drink tea." Bouhouch laughed as he interrupted Dylan's gaze. Bouhouch took a sip of tea from a small glass—also drawn from Brahim's magic bag—before handing it to Dylan.

"*Shukran,*" Dylan said. In Moroccan fashion, Brahim infused fresh mint into the hot, sugary tea. Dylan sipped from the shared glass without hesitation. *He boiled it for ten minutes.*

"Do you like it, Yusuf?" Bouhouch asked in English.

"The tea is very good," Dylan replied after his sip.

"No, Yusuf. Morocco. Bou Gafr. Our people. You are happy here?"

Berbers don't usually talk about feelings, though Bouhouch is pretty Western. How do I feel about this place? Dylan thought while pausing the conversation.

"*Ihallah*," Dylan said nodding. "*Ihallah bezzef.*"*I do like it here. I really do,* he thought.

Bouhouch repeated "*Ihallah bezzef*" for the others to hear, who then applauded.

Mumtaz, Yusuf, mumtaz!" Bouhouch said while reaching to shake Dylan's hand.

"Bouhouch," Dylan started, "how did the battle end?"

"The French had more men. The Ait 'Atta had basic rifles, but the French had machine guns and trucks. Assu u-Ba Slam surrendered, but the tribe remained free as long as they recognized the power of the new government. We remember these things today, Yusuf. And we tell our children these things. It is important." Bouhouch looked out into the distance over the precipices that sheltered his brave ancestors.

Dylan watched the sun fall low on the winter's horizon. He turned to see the gorge and surrounding hills they had to traverse in order to return. Very little of his pure water remained in his plastic bottle and the hot, sugary tea had made him thirsty. Without ceremony, the twelve made their way down the face of Bou Gafr to reconnoiter at the abandoned cement monolith below. Thirst had gripped Dylan despite his efforts to conserve his supply of clean water and his head began to pound as it had that morning. As they returned, they wound their way back through the canyon that had brought them to the great mountain. Again the men drank from the well.

"*Suw'aman*, Yusuf, *su*," Brahim said as he passed the bucket and urged Dylan to drink from the well, but Dylan could not be convinced. He had almost exhausted his own supply of water. *Dysentery or dehydration? I'll chance it with dehydration, it's not much farther.*

Dylan had lost track of time, but the sun dropped low in the winter sky, masked by the endless surrounding peaks. They returned at a much slower pace than that morning, but Dylan especially struggled to keep up. *They all walk so slow in the street but they run up and down the fucking mountains,* he thought critically. His feet were hot, sweaty, and he knew they were blistered, but he pushed on, more concerned at being lost in the dark. His shins ached with every step. He reached for his bottle. *Empty.*

"*Fuck.*" This time he said it aloud and he threw the empty bottle behind him.

"Yusuf *labas?*" Bouhouch inquired apprehensively.

"*Labas,*" he replied, without adding his thanks to God. They continued silently.

This is it. I'm going to die here. Rather than panic, however, he accepted his fate, perhaps like a ram at the point of slaughter. *This is really it.* He felt his heart pound both in his chest and in his head with every step. *Do you feel an aneurysm?*

The northward path wound its way through the hills, and Dylan could just barely see the old *hajj* in the distance. The old goat stood on a ledge and again called "yo-ho, yo-ho" over the entire valley. His voice haunted the canyon and Dylan expected wolves to respond in a chorus—the same wolves who might ultimately devour him should he fall behind. Everything—his feet, his head, and even his eyes—throbbed as he took each step.

68

He stumbled as the hike continued upwards from the valley floor. Without a flashlight, he struggled to see in the dusk. His body ached, he tasted bile, and his vision blurred. *I can't even see the path anymore. Horror.* The word resurfaced in his moment of vulnerability. In his childlike fear, the gentlest of tears spilled from the corner of his right eye as he fell. *I failed.*

Ever-resourceful Brahim saved Dylan by rustling an orange from his knapsack.

"Yusuf, *tish*," Brahim said, telling Dylan to eat and helping him to stand.

"*Shukran. Shukran bezzef* Brahim," Dylan said. He stopped, took the fruit, and devoured it, eating most of the peel, too. Reviving juice dribbled down his chin and onto his shirt; his hands became covered in a sticky mixture of sweat, pulp, and dust. Never before had he felt so savage. He bit into the orange like an apple, and he felt his hydration and energy restore as he began to once again stagger along the darkening trail.

"Yusuf *labas?*" Brahim asked.

"*Labas.*"

"*L'hamdullah,*" Brahim repeated and the men echoed. "Thanks be to God.

Eight of the troop arrived at the van as night fell. Faiz had lagged behind with some others. While they waited in the darkness of night, they busied themselves by trying to light a fire made of the scrub brush called *l-fsa*, which grew there in abundance, untouched by the grazing herds and the old women who sought it for fuel. Some men found drier bunches of the stuff and set them alight. The *l-fsa* gave off a bright flash at first but threw scant heat. A pile of three or four bunches of it made a little fire that kept them entertained but not particularly warm in the frigid night air. Above, the stars lit the sky in a way few in the modern illuminated world have seen. Stars stretched from horizon to horizon without any other light but the insignificant flame.

I am small, Dylan thought. *So very small.*

Out of the silence, the old *hajj* began to sing. Not the ululation of their advance, but a ballad. The others stood around the fragile flame and listened to the old man's hoarse voice. Bouhouch joined first, and then Brahim, and then all of the men but Dylan sang with the *hajj*. The solemn melody lasted only a moment and the group returned to the desert silence.

"What does it mean, Bouhouch?" Dylan asked, breaking the stillness.

"We are the free men, Yusuf. We are as free as the sands and the rocks of the land, and we will be sheep to no other. Not now, not ever. And our children, and theirs, will sing this song forever." The simple translation matched Dylan's Tashelheet vocabulary.

"It is beautiful, my friend," Dylan said and repeated the word for friend, "*asmuninu*."

"*Asmuninu*, Yusuf," returned Bouhouch and again the chorus of men repeated the word for friend with only the stars of the sky and the stones of the earth as their witnesses.

Midnight approached when the band of thirsty and tired men arrived in Ikniouen. The return drive had been much quieter than that of the morning. Faiz parked his van by the bakery and pushed open the sliding door for the other eleven. Despite the late hour and their fatigue, the men lingered rather than return to their homes. Again they stood in a small circle, breathing the frosty February air, their faces dimly lit by the village's sole streetlight.

"*Ar aska,*" Dylan said as he bid the group a good night.

"*Insha'Allah,*" Bouhouch reassured him, reaching for Dylan's hand.

"*Shukran.* I need sleep," Dylan said, mixing his Arabic with English. An echo of "goodnight" and handshakes came from the other men.

Dylan unlocked the heavy metal door to the stairs of his apartment and stepped in to the dark hall. He took off his Williams hat as he climbed the stairs and ran his fingers through his matted hair. *Disgusting.* When he reached the top of the stairs, he switched on the light and the sole bulb hanging from the ceiling illuminated the kitchen. Fleetingly, he looked at the phone he had left on the table—*still no messages*—and opened a bottle of clean water and began to drink. He had survived the wilderness with his two liters and Brahim's orange. Painfully removing his boots, Dylan walked to the bathroom in his socks noticing spots of blood that had seeped through the wool. He looked in the mirror above the sink and saw a filthy mess. The pipes gurgled again as he turned on the faucet: still no water. Without grumbling—like he had that morning—he washed as best he could in the cold water he kept in buckets. *I got this. I do.* The clean Boston College t-shirt and matching maroon sweatpants he put on comforted him and felt soft against his broken body; both warmed him from the chill of the apartment. *Emily*, he remembered fleetingly. He peeled off his socks and found his feet blistered with broken skin, and blood had dried on the wool. He left them bare as he hobbled across the icy cement floor to the small bedroom. He saw the bedside picture, but

71

overlooked it; he felt tired, not lonely. Switching off the light, he slipped into his cold bed on the floor piled high with thick Berber blankets. He heard the laughter of the men gathered outside, breaking the silence of the starry village night. *They are good men. Peace be upon their houses. All of them,* he said aloud before sleep gently, but swiftly, visited him.

Maryam

The full September moon almost warmed the chilly mountain air, and the bright stars and the distant blue planet pierced the dark sapphire of night as the village slept. Except for the house of Ibrahim. His wife, Fatoum, cried softly, aware more of the pain her baby would endure in its impoverished life than that of her own labor. Fatoum knew birth; indeed, while this was her ninth, only six had lived. She lay on a bed of thick Berber carpets and blankets that kept away the dampness of the earth floor. Her mother-in-law, Saida, readied the cloth with which to receive the child while water for washing, hauled by her daughter from the village tap, sat perpetually boiling on the coals of the small courtyard fire. Ibrahim tended the embers, or perhaps just played with them as a distraction. In the only other room of the earthen house, Maryam sat waiting with her three sisters and her younger brother. "Soon it will pass, little ones. Sleep," she said, enfolding them in her arms. And the full September moon continued its journey across the darkened sky until, just before the *muezzin's* cry at dawn, an undersized girl with crooked legs found her mother's embrace.

As the sun's rays broke over the imposing mountains that surrounded the village, Saida stepped into the courtyard to find

73

Ibrahim still poking at the long-cold ashes.

"Another girl. The legs are broken and she is not strong," the old woman said.

"And Fatoum?" he asked of his wife.

"She is fine and resting. Go find food at your brother's house, we have enough to do here, and all night you burned the *l-fsa* I collected yesterday. There will be no tea this morning," she said angrily as she retreated into the darkness of the salon.

"*Wa-ha*," Ibrahim said to his mother's backside as he stood and left the house.

In the sleeping room, Hassan stirred first from the pile of children that had surrounded Maryam in the night. At three, he was the youngest and busiest. In his rustling, he kicked his sister, Amina, who was less than a year older.

"Stop, Hassan," Amina complained as she awoke. She tried to nestle at Maryam's side, but the older girl woke, too. Six-year-old Aisha yawned and stretched as she opened her eyes while Heleema, eleven, spoke first.

"Is it done, Maryam? I hear nothing."

"I will see. Fetch water from the jugs and wash Hassan and Amina while I go. Aisha, you wash, too," Maryam said.

"The water is always so cold, Maryam," Heleema grumbled.

"I carry that water every day for you; be grateful, Heleema," Maryam said firmly as she bundled the damp, heavy blankets and brought them into the sunlight to dry. The warmth felt pleasant on her uncovered head as she reached toward the sky in the open courtyard. Looking at the ashes that remained in the hearth, she stirred them and kindled a fire from a few stray twigs she scrounged from the yard.

"I don't know how you do it, girl. The night fire burned everything, but you still made fire. Now we can make tea," her grandmother said from the salon doorway.

"*Salamu alaykum,*" Maryam greeted her grandmother and mother as she entered the second room. "Are you well?"

"I am well, *l'hamdullah,*" Saida curtly replied while Fatoum gently rocked her baby. The child in her arms made no sound.

"Is it a boy?" Maryam asked.

"Another girl, with broken legs. She is weak," Saida snapped. "There is much to do, girl. Begin your work, your sisters return to school today—of all days."

"The legs are different, not broken, Mama," Fatoum said softly, looking at the baby.

"*Wa-ha,*" Maryam replied, bowing to kiss her mother on the forehead and take a closer look at the little girl. "*Imzi!*" she cried, commenting on the smallness of the child.

"She is sweet, like you, Maryam," her mother said weakly and kissed the baby.

"What will she be called?" Maryam asked.

"Stupid girl," her grandmother interjected, "you know she will not be named until the seventh day. Cover your head and fetch the water, there is none left!"

"Yes, *Mahallu,*" Maryam responded to her grandmother.

"Not until seven days; that is the way of the desert," Fatoum confirmed solemnly.

Maryam left the room, littered with blankets and reeking of blood. As she again crossed the small courtyard, she saw the empty water jugs. *Every day I must fill them.*

"Heleema," she called from the door.

"*Nam?*" came the voice from the dark.

"Watch the little ones while I bring more water. Eat yester-day's bread."

"Is it a boy?" Amina asked.

"It is a girl. Let Mama rest."

"*Wa-ha*," Heleema said, now looking from the doorway into the daylight.

Maryam gathered the plastic jugs—old vegetable oil bottles—and headed for the village tap. As she walked, she passed open doorways, but few moved in that early hour that the elders referred to as "*tifout*." She had hauled water twice every day since Heleema's age and now, at seventeen, her arms and back were strong. The full jugs, which weighed thirty pounds, had always felt light to her. When she returned to their house on the edge of the village, she placed the jugs in the corner as usual and looked for the children.

"Where are Heleema and the little ones?" she asked her grandmother from the door.

"Didn't you pass them? I sent them to your uncle's. Where did you go? There is too much to do today," growled Saida. "The towels need washing, take them to the rocks. I will find *l-fsa* to burn. Every day I must find *l-fsa*."

"I went to the tap, but I did not see them; they must have gone through the *souq*. Who will stay with Mama?" Maryam asked.

"Your aunt and the others will visit soon. She will be fine, she knows childbirth."

"*Wa-ha, Mahallu*. Beware Tifigrah," Maryam cautioned her grandmother.

"He, he, he," the old woman cackled. "Tifigrah will not strike me. I am too quick for her. Now get to work, girl."

She is always mean, why can't she be nice like Mama and Baba? Maryam wondered.

Snake bites, from desert vipers and cobras, were common in the mountains among the old women like Saida who walked barefoot in search of twigs for fuel. Saida never feared the mountain menace and had never been bitten. Saida's sister, however, had died ten years earlier from a snake bite and Maryam never forgot the woman's death. Just as Maryam carried her water jugs every day, Saida also set out toward the mountains, barefoot and dressed in dark Berber layers, with only her tattooed face exposed from under her *hijab*. She moved quickly for being over sixty and took nothing with her, not even water, for the day's journey in the sun. All day she would climb into the hills in search of any twig or bit of *l-fsa* that could burn. Deforestation had plagued the tribe since they became sedentary generations before. Village elders often said that the mountains had once been covered with trees, like those in the north, but they had been cut down for fuel. The poorest, who could not afford tanks of gas, now scrounged for brush, burdening the oldest women. Yet, like most women in the mountain village, Saida accepted her work rather than bemoan it.

With Saida gone, Maryam returned to her mother and new sister in the earthen-floored salon.

"*Labas?*" she asked as she entered.

"*Kulshi labas, l'hamdullah.* Your sister is also well," Fatoum said faintly.

"Thanks be to God. I will wash the cloths as *Mahallu* said. Heleema took the children to Auntie's so you can rest."

"Good. You must also take the herd today, Maryam. Heleema returns to school like Aisha. I know it will make more work for you, but it must be done," her mother explained. "Your father has decided it."

"*Wa-ha,*" Maryam responded rather than argue with her mother about the considerable change in her daily duties. *I hate the old goat Taggat*, she thought as she turned to leave. *But it must be done, Baba has said.* She kissed her mother and the infant, tied the bundle of dirty towels to her back, and set off toward the rocks where a tiny pool of muddy water—shared by the poorest women of the village—survived in the arid desert.

Ibrahim had surprised the family earlier that summer when he announced that Heleema would return to school after the August holiday. He said the young American and the new village head-master had convinced him and some of the other men to send their girls to the new middle school. Like Maryam, Heleema stopped attending school after the compulsory primary years. For the last year-and-a-half, Heleema had taken the herd into the hills every day, allowing Maryam to learn more domestic skills in the hope of a proposal. An offer of marriage for her, they all knew, was unlikely, in part because the poor family could not afford a dowry, and also because they had darker skin than most Berbers. The family was *haratin*—Africans once considered slaves among the Berber tribes—and while over the centuries they had assimilated into the tribe, the color of their skin and their poverty still set them apart. When Maryam turned sixteen, Ibrahim had lost hope of marrying her to someone in the village. Sending Heleema to school might increase the likelihood of the younger daughter's marriage prospects. Maryam would again care for the goats when school began. Maryam never protested; as with all things, she accepted what others decided for her.

"Waaa Usted!" Smail and his two friends yelled from across the dirt road to Dylan's open window. *I really will miss them calling me teacher,* he thought as he walked down the stairs and pulled open the heavy metal door, stepping into the morning sun, and greeting the boys with a round of high fives.

"Andu sa madras?" he asked, wondering if they would accom-

pany him to school.

"Wa-ha" they replied, again giggling as they followed him into the warren behind the house. He gave them each a fruit-flavored candy bought from Brahim's *hanoot.*

"Shukran bezzef, Usted," the youngest, Mohammed, thanked Dylan before hopping off the stoop and following him into the warren of ramshackle dwellings behind the village road. Although it was the first day of a new school year, nothing seemed extraordinary to them—the boys wore the same clothes as always, and they carried nothing special for school. They practiced their Arabic numbers with Dylan as they walked, just as they often had before.

"Wahid, joojz, tleta..." they counted, still laughing as they passed the solitary house of Ibrahim. From the outside, it looked like the other houses with its earthen walls and corrugated roofs. Rocks, unused cinder blocks, and trash littered the area around the house; the scene was familiar for this—the poorest—part of the village. The metal door stood cracked ajar.

"Tarbet tujdit," Smail whispered, mentioning the new girl while pointing to the door.

"Yeah?" Dylan asked. He knew the family expected a baby but did not know how soon. "When? Last night?" he asked the boys in Tashelheet.

"Yeah," Mohammed nodded.

Dylan counted the girls aloud from memory. *"Hamsa?"* he asked, raising five fingers.

"Yeah," Smail confirmed. *"Bezzef!"*

Dylan laughed. Five girls probably seemed like a lot to young Smail.

The four continued walking toward the schools through the warren, where the haphazard arrangement of earth and stone houses lacked order. Like the house of Ibrahim, they were comprised of two rooms connected by an open-air courtyard and, while a few of them enjoyed electricity, none had running water. Most village women, like Maryam, only walked through the warren and were rarely, if ever, seen on the main village road. Dylan liked walking there both because it provided the most direct route to the schools and it reminded him how most people in the village lived. Making their way around the houses, Dylan saw Ibrahim and his brother Ahmed standing outside the latter's house.

"*Salamu alaykum,* Sidi Ibrahim," Dylan greeted him with a handshake.

"*Wa alaykum salam*, Yusuf. *Labas?*" Ibrahim replied.

"*Kulshi labas, l'hamdulillah.* Sidi Ahmed, *labas?*" Dylan asked as the trio exchanged the ritual greeting. "*M'bruk!*" Dylan congratulated them on the birth.

"*Shukran,*" Ibrahim nodded, looking downward.

"Is it a girl?" Dylan asked to be polite.

"It is," Ahmed confirmed with a nod.

"*Mezyan,*" Dylan affirmed, but Ibrahim made no acknowledgment. "Heleema will go to school today?"

"She just left the house. She will arrive soon, *insha'Allah,*" Ibrahim responded.

"*Mezyan,*" Dylan repeated.

"*Andu?*" Young Smail asked if Dylan wanted to go and poked at his arm. The boys were bored by the adult conversation.

"*Andu,*" Dylan said to the boys, resuming his walk toward the school. He looked back to Ibrahim and Ahmed, waved, and again congratulated them with: "*M'bruk.*"

"*Waaa Usted,*" Smail called to Dylan as they approached the primary school.

"*Waaa Smail!*" Dylan returned.

"When do you go to America?" Smail asked in Tashelheet.

"The day after tomorrow, *insha'Allah.*"

"*Insha'Allah. Ihallah,*" Smail affirmed it was good, and the boys echoed.

"*Ihallah,*" Dylan agreed. He left the boys at the primary school and parted with more high fives. "*Ar men bed, asmunink,*" calling them friends and hoping to see them later.

"*Insha'Allah, Usted,*" they giggled as they hurried into the courtyard as their teacher rang the handbell—the time being after 9:30. *They call me teacher even though I'm not really. Maybe I'll teach when I go back home.* Dylan waved at the young man ringing the bell and continued walking up the hill on the main road toward the middle school. He saw Heleema and four girls enter the courtyard ahead. *Good*, he said softly, *she went.*

School and girls, he mused. *We forget, back home, that the chance is so limited in these places. Aly needs to finish high school and stop complaining about it. Kayla, I bet, is doing great in law school. I know she'll advocate for girls like Heleema and her friends. The world needs her and she'll do great things.* The corner of his mouth tugged at a smile as he continued to walk to the middle school.

Dylan had undertaken some worthwhile projects in the second year of his Peace Corps service, and he had some more undeveloped ideas as his service drew to a close. He had worked with Sidi Lahcen, the new headmaster of the middle school, to encourage rural fathers like Ibrahim to keep their daughters in school. Six girls, including Heleema, had re-enrolled that term to resume their studies. Dylan had also helped the local civic association implement a nascent waste management program. Also, he had recruited young Amir, Bouhouch's nephew, to coach soccer games for Smail and the boys. Sometimes Dylan played in the matches, too. After a difficult start of frustration and loneliness in his first year of service, Dylan had found his place in the village and became nostalgic as he approached the middle school for his last day of work. *It's been good for me here. Surprisingly good.*

After an hour's walk to the rocks the village women called *izran*, Maryam let the bundle tied to her back fall to the ground. The heavy blankets and the make-shift pack gave Maryam no support, so she felt relief when she straightened her back. The slow water—always shallow and muddy—barely trickled after the dry summer. Without a tap at home, the poorest women of the village could only wash their laundry at the rocks. Maryam scrubbed the bloody towels, working hard to get the thin cloths clean in the puddle of water and then beat them against the rocks. The harder she worked, the more water flowed generously from the rocks, easing her work and making her smile. *Ihallah*, she said to herself, *it is good*. The sun—which they called Tafouit—blazed strong but did not weaken her as she worked. Focused on her washing, she did not notice Igdi the dog approach, panting.

"Stupid girl, you've ruined the little water with soap. So stupid," the dog barked.

"There is plenty of fresh water here by the rock that I've not touched. Come, drink," she replied without looking up.

"Stupid girl," Igdi repeated as he limped toward the rock. Igdi always limped around the outskirts of the village. No one knew from where he came, and he fed on the few scraps he could scrounge. Rarely did villagers have scraps of food, but somehow he survived.

"Are you so mean to the other village girls, Igdi?" she asked.

"Stupid girl, you know you're the only one who can talk to me," barked the dog.

"Drink. The cool water will make you feel better, Igdi," she said.

"Why do you care?" he asked as he lapped the cool, fresh water near the stone.

"No one should thirst, not even a dog like you," she said as she worked.

"Stupid girl," he growled as he turned and limped away.

Igdi is always so angry, his leg must hurt, she reasoned. *I would be angry if I limped.*

She arranged the cloths on the rocks to dry in the warm sun. Her hands had wrinkled from the soapy water, but she did not tire. She looked at Tafouit overhead. *Midday. Taggat will be hungry if I don't take the herd to eat soon*, she thought as she stood up to return to the house, leaving the cloths to dry. *There's always more work to do.*

She walked more quickly without the bundle tied to her back. Looking at the hard desert floor as she moved, she smiled when she noticed the absence of her shadow. *Tafouit may be strong for the others, but she does not harm me. Why?* No one had ever told her why she could make fire with so little *l-fsa*, or make water flow from the rocks, or walk without a shadow, or talk to animals. *But why am I different? I will ask Mama.*

Amina and Hassan sat in the courtyard; Maryam patted them each on the head as she walked passed and into the salon. Four women, including her aunt, gathered with Fatoum and the quiet baby. They snacked on almonds and dates harvested from far oases. Maryam greeted the women and ate a date but did not sit.

"I will take the goats now, Mama."

"*Shukran*, Maryam," Fatoum thanked her while discretely nursing the baby.

"The goats are hungry, Maryam. They made an awful noise this morning when the children left for school. I told the men to be sure nothing was the matter," her aunt said. Ibrahim was too poor to own his own goats. He survived as something of a blacksmith, but people now replaced his crude work with new, machine-made materials easily brought from Boumalne. The two men agreed many years earlier that Ahmed would pay for and keep the herd while Ibrahim and his daughters would tend them. The families shared the meat.

"*Wa-ha*, Mama," Fatoum said, kissing the hands of her mother and aunt before ducking out of the dark salon into the brightness of day. Again, she stretched toward the sky, straightening her back and inhaling a deep breath before departing for the goat pen.

I will not marry like Mama or Auntie, she thought as she neared the corral. *I have nothing to give like the other girls.* Out of frustration, she picked up a pebble and threw it ahead toward the goat pen, falling short. *But it is good, Mama needs me. The little ones need me. The goats need me.* As Maryam approached the enclosure, the goats bleated.

"The pretty one is at school today. The old, ugly one is back; no one will marry her," said Taggat, the oldest of the she-goats. The others bleated in agreement.

"*Y'allah* Taggat. *Andu*," Maryam responded, paying the beast little attention as she opened the flimsy gate of corrugated metal.

"We want the pretty one," Taggat said, refusing to move.

"Come, or you will starve."

"We'll starve anyway," a dirty black billy goat said. "You

know there's no grass."

"I will find grass for you," Maryam said and clicked her teeth to push the goats along. Taggat bleated and walked out of the pen as the others followed.

Just as the encroaching Sahara made timber painfully scarce for the Ait 'Atta tribe of the Saghro mountains, generations of grazing had also made pasturing their small herds difficult. Only a few members of the tribe remained nomads, and their small caravans traveled through the village each spring and fall on their way to and from the green fields of Azilal in the north. People like Ibrahim and his family, however, had settled and scrounged on the little *l-fsa* that grew within walking distance of the village. The thin and sickly herd never grew strong with their meager diet.

"The ugly girl who is too stupid to go to school says she will bring us to the grassy land today," Taggat announced to the small herd while taunting Maryam.

"I will bring you to grass and water, Taggat, a place where Heleema never thought to look. *Y'allah*," she said as she threw another stone toward them. They walked toward the east with the massive ridge to their right and Tafouit just behind them in the sky.

"When will the smart, pretty girl come back? After you marry?" Taggat taunted.

"Shut up," Maryam said and kicked a bit of dust at her, startling the rest who began to prance. Taggat bleated and pushed out her tongue as she trotted ahead toward the hills.

Unlike her grandmother, Maryam feared walking barefoot in the hills. Plastic shoes were inexpensive to buy at *souq*, but their cheap quality made them cut the women's feet and many preferred to go barefoot. While antivenom was available throughout the kingdom, the Ministry of Health decided that the Boumalne clinic would serve as the local dispensary; patients would have to go there when bit. Many died along the two-hour journey on the mountain road. Despite the discomfort of the cheap shoes, Maryam wore them for fear of the snakes, but they pinched her feet as she walked.

Again, Maryam cast no shadow in Tafouit's gaze nor did the heat, although never searing at that elevation, bother her. *What's beyond the far mountains?* She looked back at the jagged landscape beyond the village and thought of her brother. *Omar crosses the mountains to go to Marrakech. Baba sent him to work, but Baba would never send me—he says it is too dangerous for a girl like me. The teacher went to university in the city and she is a woman. But she is Arab, not Tamazight.*

"You will never know what it is like," bleated Taggat, interrupting her thoughts.

"The road to Boumalne goes through those mountains. Omar now lives in the city beyond the mountains. Baba said Heleema might one day go over the mountains, too, now that she returns to school."

"Even I have been over the mountains," said Taggat. "Your father took me from the big *souq* by van, stupid girl. You have always stayed here."

"One day I will go with Heleema, but only to Boumalne. Not to the city with Omar. It is good for me to stay here with Mama and the little ones."

Taggat bleated and Maryam threw another stone to push the herd along toward the hard nothingness littered with rocks that stretched out before them.

From his small, open window, Dylan watched Maryam and

the goats become smaller as she neared the distant hills. *So sad*, he thought, *there's nothing for them. What will become of her? Of these people?* He watched her disappear behind the hill and turned his attention inside. The apartment was mostly packed since he was leaving the day after tomorrow. Brahim the storekeeper had bought the plastic table and chairs, his mattress, and the foam sofa. A Berber carpet—made by Bouhouch's mother—stuffed almost all of his pack. To make room for it, he would leave most of his clothes to young Amir, the baker's son. He gave Bouhouch the few books and things he had collected in his two years. Little remained in the hollow, cement space, except the picture of Kayla and Aly that he kept by his bedside with his phone. For months, the picture lay buried under his thick new copy of *Harry Potter*. Aly, he knew, thrived as she started college and they still talked on most Sundays. They had discussed seeing each other in the coming weeks.

Passing over the picture, he reached for his phone and, out of boredom, scrolled through the call log:

```
Kayla(2)  08/APR/2008
USA       03:26
```

She hadn't answered at first.

Five months later and she doesn't know I'm headed home soon.

"Hey Dyl. Everything ok?" she had asked.

"Yeah. Good. Happy Easter."

"Same to you. Not like you to do Easter."

"Yeah, I guess. I'm in Marrakech for the weekend with some other volunteers. It's the closest place with a church. There's a nice old priest, from Boston actually."

"Wow. You and church."

"Yup."

"How's law school?" he continued, breaking the pause that had developed.

"Hard. I think I'm getting it. How are things there? Is it hot?"

"Not yet, though it's never too hot in the mountains. It's good—really good. Just another season."

"I'm glad Dyl. Really."

"Thanks. Me, too. For you, I mean. Hey, maybe when I get back this fall, you know, we…"

"Dyl. I'm not so sure I'll be around in the fall, with clerking and all. I gotta go though, ok? It was really good hearing from you. I'm glad you're well. Really."

"K. Happy Easter."

"Yeah. Happy Easter, Dyl."

That was the end. And he knew it, both outside the Holy Martyrs church in Marrakech, the city where his great adventure started, and later in his Ikniouen apartment. *Goodbye, Kayla.*

Dylan turned to the open window, unsure whether he would cry or not. The September days shortened and the light struck the distant mountains earlier, turning the Sahara from its washed appearance to a deeper russet hue. A motorcycle sputtered below. *Probably Brahim making a delivery to some distant outpost.* The thought of Brahim pleased him, and he thought back to the time, not long after the Bou Gafr trek, when he baked an apple pie for Bouhouch, Brahim, and Faiz. After eating Moroccan food for a year, Dylan thought it only fitting to serve his friends something classically American. He noticed the empty dish in a pile on the counter. His three friends had all hated eating the pie in his small kitchen.

"Yusuf, there is not enough sugar in this," Bouhouch had protested.

"There's half a cone!"

"We thank you, Yusuf, and now we know why you are so thin. Meskeen Yusuf!" Bouhouch teased. The other two men erupted into laughter at the word *meskeen*.

The susurrus of the breeze brought Dylan's attention back to the window. Pushing his face out of the screenless opening, he felt the pleasing experience of the warm sun and cool wind. Near the eastern hills, a bent-over figure moved with a brisk pace toward the village. The sight looked familiar to him, although he did not recognize Saida. *Where do they find the stuff?* he asked himself as he shook his head. *There are no trees for miles and yet every day they find twigs to burn for the night. I wish I could have fixed that problem,* he thought as he closed the window and flicked on the light in his dim apartment.

The September moon, now slightly less than full, again lit the slumbering village. The stars and planets, too, stood sentinel over the once-nomadic tribe and especially the quiet baby with crooked legs. Fatoum remained in the cold salon and tried to nurse the child who ate little while Saida snored in the dark corner, tired from her day's journey beyond the village. Ibrahim returned home for Maryam's couscous but slept at Ahmed's once he found everything in order under his roof. Across the courtyard, Maryam gathered Heleema, Aisha, Amina, and Hassan together having washed them in the water she hauled that day.

"Why does the baby not cry?" Aisha asked. "Hassan cried so much as a baby."

"She is happy. Hassan was never happy," Maryam said, touching the boy's nose and making Heleema and Aisha giggle.

"Mama makes better couscous than you," Amina complained,

seeking attention.

"Go to sleep, Amina," said Heleema, who also competed for Maryam's attention. Hassan yawned and stretched himself across his sisters, while Amina turned away and closed her eyes, leaving the older girls—Aisha and Heleema—awake with Maryam.

"Did you like school, Heleema?" Maryam whispered so as not to distract the others.

"Arabic and French are hard. I wish they spoke Tashelheet as we do."

Maryam had also learned a little Arabic and French in primary school but only spoke the Berber dialect since leaving primary school. Since she only spoke to the women of the village, and her family had neither electricity nor a television, any language but Tashelheet proved useless to Maryam. "How are your numbers?" she asked.

"Good. The other girls are smarter because I missed two years. It will be difficult."

"I loved the numbers. And languages. And the Qur'an. School is good for you, Heleema. One day," Maryam assured her, "it will be well, *insha'Allah*."

"One day, *insha'Allah*," Aisha repeated, trying to mimic her sister's confidence.

Maryam yawned like Hassan and stretched out on the damp carpet. The girls rested their heads on her as they warmed each other under the blankets. Only the light of the September moon shone through the open courtyard door as sleep again visited the house.

"That girl never cries and she's not eating. We should call the midwife," Saida said as she folded the last of her blankets in the early morning light.

"Tomorrow, *insha'Allah*," Fatoum said, kissing the infant's head. "She is peaceful."

"*Insha'Allah*," Saida repeated as she stepped into the courtyard, shooing Amina and Hassan out of the doorway by clapping her hands. "Eat your bread and leave your mother."

Maryam finished feeding the children while Heleema readied herself for school. Amina and Hassan looked inquisitively into the dark salon where they could just barely see their mother holding the baby, but they kept their distance for fear of their grandmother.

"Send the little ones to your aunt while Heleema is away. You must take the goats, but there is no washing today," Saida reminded Maryam. "That weak baby takes too much of your mother's strength. We never have enough to burn for tea."

"*Wa-ha*. Be careful, *Mahallu*," Maryam replied as barefoot Saida left for the hills.

"I am fine," the old woman said, not bothering to turn back to her granddaughter.

She didn't need to remind me about the goats. Thank God there is no more scrubbing today and I don't have to see her until dark, Maryam thought as the old woman hastened toward the hills.

The four younger children set out for their uncle's house led by Heleema.

"Be good for Auntie," Maryam said firmly to Amina and Hassan from the open door. "Be clever in school, girls," she encouraged Aisha and Heleema.

"When will Mama make couscous again? I don't like yours," Amina complained.

"Shush, Amina," Maryam scolded. "Mama and the baby must rest, and you eat too much couscous anyway. Now go," she said, closing the metal door.

Maryam returned to her mother in the quiet and dark room.

"You are well?" Maryam asked.

"I am, God be praised. And your sister is well, thanks be to God."

"You should walk, Mama. Give me the child and stand."

"*Wa-ha,*" Fatoum said without fuss. Maryam helped remove the thick blankets that covered her mother. Handing one daughter to the other, Fatoum slowly stood.

"You look weak, Mama. I will make you tea."

Fatoum consented as she shuffled into the warm sunlight of the courtyard. Maryam looked down at the small, tightly-wrapped bundle of her sister. Even in the dark room she could see that the baby's eyes were closed and hear her labored breathing. The child seemed smaller than her siblings and her chin looked different, too. *Tiny. Too tiny.* With the baby in her arms, she fed the hearth with what she found, again making fire from almost nothing.

"Mama, should we fetch the midwife to see the baby?" Maryam asked as she set the kettle on the fire. Just enough water remained in the jugs to fill the kettle.

"Tomorrow, *insha'Allah.* Today you must take the goats and I will rest with the girl."

"*Wa-ha*, Mama. The girl is in God's hands," Maryam said, holding the baby.

"This little one is different, Maryam. Just like you; you are different. All will be well with her as it is for you," Fatoum said as she gently took back the baby from Maryam. For the first time, Fatoum acknowledged Maryam's difference.

"Why am I different, Mama? What does it mean?" her voice trembled.

"It means that God has been good to you, as you are good to us all, Maryam."

"But why? I want to be like the other girls, Mama."

"It is the way of the desert, Maryam. *Ihallah*."

"*Wa-ha* Mama. *Wa-ha*." Maryam agreed gently without asking more.

After only a few minutes in the sun and a few sips of hot tea, Fatoum settled herself in the salon with the baby while Maryam tidied the courtyard and swept the dirt floor with a reed brush. She ended her daily chores by folding the blankets and fetching more water.

"Mama, I must leave you to take the goats. Will you be well?" Maryam asked.

"I will, child. You are a blessing to your mother," Fatoum said. As she smiled, deep wrinkles formed her dark and tattooed careworn face. Yet, even in the privacy of the salon with her daughter, Fatoum kept her head wrapped with a *hijab*.

Maryam nodded in acknowledgment and left the house for her errand. Walking alone to the pen, she looked down and, again not seeing her shadow, looked up at bright Tafouit in the sky. "Why must it be me? Taggat is so mean to me."

"Your mother told you. You are different," the sun answered with a woman's voice.

"But why?" Maryam persisted.

"It is the way of it the desert." Tafouit said no more.

"The ugly one has returned, and the pretty one has gone to school again," Taggat bleated to the others as Maryam approached.

Maryam ignored her as she opened the gate. The goats were playful with each other and trotted toward the eastern hills. A small kid goat—Maryam called him Uli—nibbled on a black plastic bag stuck under a rock. Maryam gently tossed a small stone to urge Uli along. Steering around the village edge, they traveled on worn footpaths always strewn with litter. *There's nothing here*, Maryam said to herself. On the village outskirts, they passed a few small fields with onions and corn stalks—tired crops grown from exhausted soil—that both the goats and Maryam knew better than to touch. Beyond the small patches of farmland grew a spot of tall, thin grass littered with stones. They also knew better than to enter this space—this was the burial ground. No one ever stopped there to remember, and Maryam kept moving the goats toward the hills. *Only the men go there to bury the dead*, she thought. *We are not welcome there.*

Only the outcast Igdi lurked in the tall grass of the cemetery where others feared to walk. He emerged from the tall grass and startled Uli, before limping toward Maryam.

"Now with the goats instead of the washing? Where is your pretty sister?"

"She is at school, Igdi," Maryam said keeping her focus ahead toward the hills.

"Yes, she is. I saw her walking there this morning. Poor you are back with the goats," Igdi barked coyly. Maryam threw a rock that grazed a good leg and he growled.

"Igdi, why do you limp?" she asked. The dog looked away and scanned the area with his eyes before turning back to her.

"Tifigrah. She bit me but could not kill me. The wound will not heal after many years. Beware of her, for you and Taggat are not as strong as I am," he said and retired to the tall grass of the burial ground.

Tafouit slowly moved overhead as they walked. *Shadows follow the goats, but not me*, Maryam observed. *Like Mama said, I am different.*

The goats bleated as Taggat snapped: "You always bring us to the east, but there is nothing to eat here, stupid girl."

"I brought you here yesterday and you had plenty, old goat."

The black billy turned to old Taggat and said, "She's right. Only she brings us to the grass. With the other, it's always *l-fsa*, and very far away. This one is better, now shut up."

Taggat stuck out her tongue and Maryam threw another stone to again move the herd toward a nearby gully. The flat, stony earth across which they walked had cracked long ago from the mighty Tafouit. As they approached the gully, sprouts of green grass suddenly became visible above the banks of the *oued*. The small, but full, river sliced the parched earth in two. The goats—Taggat included—ran toward the secluded oasis. Tafouit continued her march overhead, but Maryam did not feel her rays as she sat contentedly in the oasis, watching the goats have their fill of green grass and cool water.

Dylan was not expected at the school on his last day in the village, but he visited again to say goodbye. He bade his farewells as he walked, lingering where he once raced.

"*Salamu alaykum, Hajj*," he said to the old man who had led him to Bou Gafr.

"*Wa alaykum salam*, Yusuf," the man said, touching his hand to his heart.

"*Salaam*, Sidi Mohammed," he greeted another man.

"*Bonjour*, Yusuf."

His greetings continued as he made his way to the school one last time, but not before paying one final visit to Abdullah to give back his post office box key. He turned right at the lamppost to enter the office. Since it was Thursday and not *souq* day, the cement room was empty except for Abdullah.

"Mister Yusuf has no mails today," Abdullah said to him before Dylan could insert his key into the box. "You will return to America tomorrow?"

"*Insha'Allah*," he said, stepping toward the mail counter. This was not entirely true, he still had to go through exit formalities in Rabat, but tomorrow was an easier explanation given the persistent limitations of his vocabulary.

"*Insha'Allah*. We wishes you, and your father, and your mother, and your sister all to have health," the postmaster said.

"*Shukran*. Thanks be to God," Dylan said, putting his hand to his heart.

"We, Yusuf, are friends," Abdullah said, extending his hand.

Dylan received his hand, and both men enfolded the hand-shake with their left hands.

"*Asmuninu*, Sidi Abdullah," Dylan said, using the Tashelheet word for friend.

"*Asmuninu*, Sidi Yusuf."

Dylan placed both his hands over his heart and backed away from the counter feeling his eyes water before turning toward the sun outside.

"*Bon voyage*, Dy-lan," and Abdullah waved goodbye.

Dylan changed his clothes to set out for a final, solitary hike in the perfect late-summer afternoon. He had, in that last year, built up a good endurance as he explored the surrounding mountains. Sometimes Smail and his friends would hike along for a few yards, laughing as they went, but Dylan would quickly outpace them as he headed east. He passed the small farm plots—*never sustainable*, he thought—and then the cemetery. He had once, unknowingly, walked through the tall grass of the cemetery instead of around it, and an observant tribesman later rebuked him for the mistake.

As he walked briskly on the dirt trail and approached the waterless banks of the *oued*, he saw Maryam and her small herd of sickly goats. The girl sat on the hard sand while the goats seemed to push at stones and kick-up dirt in search of anything green. *Her life is so sad*, he thought. *What will become of her without school or marriage? Maybe it will be better for Heleema now that she has returned to school, but what about Maryam? God will take care of her. Like Kayla.*

Dylan rambled past Maryam unnoticed, and he made no effort to gain her attention. The terrain now appeared familiar to him, like home. On the path ahead, he noticed an odd shape and slowed down. He studied the apparent pile from a distance and it seemed as though someone had placed stones in the middle of the path. The scene confused him, and as he walked toward it, he found that it looked less like a pile of rocks. He picked up a stone and threw it at the pile, causing it to come alive and straighten. *Snake.* They were common enough in the mountains, and he avoided watching it slither away. *I won't miss that,* he thought as he turned back toward the village. He could see Smail and the others playing soccer closer to the village. *I'll join them*, he thought and jogged a little faster toward them.

Sitting by the stream, Maryam thought of the baby. *So small.*

"You will have no children," Taggat scowled as she looked up from the clear water. "You're too old and too ugly. Your father sent the pretty one to school and sent you back to take care of us. Stupid girl."

Maryam threw another rock but intentionally overshot the old goat.

"Don't listen to Taggat," said the black billy. "You'll eat her

97

soon enough." He bleated and the others echoed in agreement. Taggat turned and walked away from the herd, toward the far bank of the *oued*.

Again, Maryam stared at the surrounding mountains. *What is over there? Where is the city where Omar lives?* she wondered. She lowered her head and adjusted her *hijab.*

"Do you wish to go to school like your sister?" the billy asked.

"I am too old. Who would feed you if I went to school?"

"It is true," the billy admitted.

"Mama needs me. It is the way of the desert," she said, both to herself and the goat. "I am not like the others." She tossed a stone into the water, emitting a sigh and nodding in disappointment as the billy returned to grazing.

Little Uli first leaped in fright, and then the others. Something had moved at the far end of the oasis and the startled kid splashed through the river. The other goats, along with Maryam, turned to look. Taggat stood near Uli, but saw no danger. Confused, Maryam stood to see better, throwing a stone at Taggat to draw her back into the fold.

"*Y'allah, andu,*" Maryam said, trying to move them back toward the village. For once, Taggat cooperated and started to rejoin the group. Taking a step away from the water's edge, the old goat froze and bleated in pain.

"What's wrong, old thing?" asked Maryam. Then she saw her—Tifigrah—releasing her bite from Taggat's hind leg and silently slithering back into the oasis grass. Taggat stumbled forward into the water while the others remained immobilized.

"I am fine," Taggat bleated. "The cruel dog lives and so will I. Come, let's go," she said breathlessly while limping toward Maryam and the others.

They returned toward the village pushed along by Maryam

from behind. The goats trotted apprehensively, and Maryam scanned every step of the way with wide eyes, but the danger of Tifigrah had passed. Taggat, however, lagged behind the herd. She bleated when she stumbled and Maryam turned back.

"Come now, old thing, we're almost there."

"Stupid ugly girl, let me be. The dog lives and so will I," Taggat bleated as she struggled for breath. Maryam knew that death hovered over the old goat. The family would not be able to eat the meat and the loss would be significant.

They were close enough to the village that Maryam could have sent her father to finish Taggat while she returned the other seven. But she did not. She tried to lift the old beast onto her shoulders with her strength, but Taggat fought her.

"Leave me, stupid girl, that hurts," Taggat bit at Maryam.

"Stop, I will carry you," Maryam said. Yet, despite all of Maryam's strength, Taggat would not be carried, nor would she walk any farther. Maryam sat down on the hard, dusty ground, and settled the beast in her lap. The hind leg oozed and bled, the goat's filthy fur smelled, but none of this bothered Maryam. She sat peacefully while the rest of the herd looked on from a distance—they had never seen such a thing before. Maryam stroked the head of old Taggat while the goat's breathing became shallow until it stopped.

The billy broke the silence.

"It is the way of the desert, girl," he said. "Leave her and we will return to the village. There is nothing to do."

"I should have watched more carefully and warned her."

"You could not have warned her. It is the way of the desert. Come, child."

Maryam stayed, holding the animal. She sat there, without a

shadow, stroking the mangy fur of the old goat while Tafouit continued on her westward journey. Rather than wander, the other goats watched Maryam sit on the hamada with the dead animal.

"Stupid girl, what are you doing?"

Maryam looked down at Taggat, but the animal had stopped moving. The familiar voice belonged neither to Taggat nor Igdi. *Who speaks to me?*

"Get up. What is this?" Saida's hunched shadow fell on Maryam.

"The old goat is dead, *Mahallu*."

"I see, but why do you hold the beast? Move the herd before night falls, stupid girl."

Maryam unceremoniously left Taggat where they had sat, her lip only slightly trembling and her eyes misting despite the dryness of the desert.

"Don't be stupid, girl. We should have eaten her last year, now she is wasted."

Hiding her melancholy, Maryam told her grandmother about the snake.

"Tifigrah is so dangerous, *Mahallu*. You must be careful in the desert."

"A danger only for the slow and the weak, like the goat. Now hurry, you should have returned long ago—there is much to do for your mother and that sick child," she said as they parted, with Saida returning to the house and Maryam herding the goats to the pen.

"No one ever knows when Tifigrah will strike, girl," the billy said to Maryam as he entered the pen. Maryam nodded. Uli brushed along her side and bleated.

"You are different than your sister. You will make us strong with your grass and your water," Uli said, prancing.

"*Insha'Allah,*" Maryam laughed.

By the time she returned home, her grandmother had already told Ibrahim what had happened and where the animal lay. Knowing that the venom had spoiled the meat, he left it to be taken by the desert itself. Maryam prepared the couscous while Hassan sat by the small fire playing with an empty plastic bag. As dusk came, the *muezzin* called the faithful to their evening prayers, Tafouit sank below the mountains, and the stars and planets became bright in the evening sky. The baby's second day ended.

The waning September moon illuminated the cold desert as the scavengers tore apart Taggat's tired old body. Igdi, too, grinned as he bit into the goat's flesh; he had survived the wrath of Tifigrah while the goat perished. *The mountains are no place for the weak*, he growled as he limped away, having tasted flesh.

Moonlight streamed in the doorway of the salon where Fatoum remained with the infant. The girl had not eaten in many hours and her heartbeat felt irregular as Fatoum held the baby close to her breast. Fatoum had known from birth the fate of this little one. Perhaps it was the crooked legs, or perhaps it was just her maternal instinct. Rather than summon the midwife or doctor, Fatoum simply held her baby for the last two days, waiting until the prescribed seventh day to name her, always keeping the child close to her heart.

Again, Saida snored in the corner while Ibrahim sat awake by the struggling fire. Maryam entered the dark salon a final time before putting the children to bed.

"Stay, Maryam, just for a little while."

"*Wa-ha*, Mama," she said as she sat down next to her mother

101

and baby sister in the calmness of the night; calm, not still because of Saida's snoring and the crackle of the fire, but because serenity enveloped their small, desert house.

"What will she be called, Mama?" Maryam asked, pulling the blanket to see her sister.

"She will not live, Maryam. Like the other two. That is the way of the desert."

A tear, caught in the moonlight of the open door, rolled down Maryam's face.

"I will get the doctor, Mama. I will wake him. I will go now," she said, struggling to stand. Fatoum calmly shook her head.

"The time has already passed, Maryam. The angel has taken her. Be at peace."

Knowing this to be true, Maryam sat with her mother, who now held two daughters in her arms. In Maryam's absence, Heleema would settle the others while Ibrahim again kept vigil by the small courtyard fire.

Tradition dictated that the child not be named for seven days because death lurked so closely in the mountains. "That is the way of the desert," her mother had said, both this time and the times before. Maryam grieved so profoundly, perhaps because she could be a mother herself and yet had no prospect of such a life. While holding a lifeless child, Fatoum reached to Maryam and kissed her grown daughter on the forehead.

"God is great, little one. God is great," she said. Maryam cried gently with her mother and watched for dawn.

Dylan took one last look around the bare apartment, feeling both excited to return home and sad to leave his newfound life in Ikniouen behind. He flashed on the Nokia phone: 5:28. *Still too early*, he thought. *Take one last look from the roof.* Again he put his Williams ball cap over his brown disheveled hair as he climbed the stairs to the top. The moon hung low in the sky but the village remained in darkness. A fair breeze carried the smell of smoke from small hearth fires. The only light came from the sole street lamp near the post office, not the darkened houses. *I never understood why they put a light there. There's so much about this place that I'll never understand. I suppose that's just the way of it here.* He pulled from his pocket the photograph of Kayla and his sister, which had resurfaced as he packed his things. *I don't need this anymore, I'll see Aly soon,* he thought as he let the mountain wind carry the picture over the sleeping village, disappearing into the morning light the elders called *tifout. The horror of night gives way to the light of day. I must have read that somewhere—it's deep shit. But true, I think.* He caught his last glimpse of the photograph blowing toward the small house of Ibrahim. *God will take care of them,* he said softly to the fading stars. *God will take care of them all, insha'Allah.*

The eastern sky grew bright, signaling the time for Dylan's departure. He took a final look and whispered *b'slama* before he descended to the van below. When he opened the door and stepped out into the dark, he saw a small crowd of men standing around the old white van waiting to depart. Faiz took Dylan's pack and tied it to the roof while the other men offered him the front passenger's seat. There were many ritual greetings, handshakes, and even hugs among the men before Faiz opened the driver's door, said *"Y'allah,"* and tooted the horn.

"Yusuf, *andu?"* Faiz asked Dylan, as he had that day in Boumalne two years before.

"Andu," Dylan replied, nodding at the kind face of his friend.

"Wa-ha," Faiz said shifting the van into gear. Before he released the brake, Dylan heard a knock on his window. Dylan

turned to see Brahim and Bouhouch.

"Yusuf!" they said as he rolled down the window. "You go?"

"Bouhouch! Brahim!" he exclaimed with genuine joy. "Yes. I go back to America." Dylan had repeatedly said goodbye to them over the previous days, so they were not surprised. They reached into the van and took both of his hands.

"We are friends, Yusuf. Always. As we say, *lla yrhn l-walidin*. Peace to you, your father, your mother, and your family. Peace, my friend," Bouhouch said, blessing Dylan.

"*Shukran. Walidina u walidik,*" Dylan returned the blessing.

"*Ayhulf rbbi,* Yusuf," Brahim said quietly.

"Do you know what it means? It is another saying of ours," Bouhouch explained.

"I do not, my Tashelheet is still *meskeen.*"

"Brahim has said 'May God give back to you everything you have given to us.'"

"*Shukran, asmuninu,*" Dylan responded, trying to think of the plural form of "friends" but once again fell short in his Tashelheet. "I will return, one day," he said in Berber.

"*Insha'Allah,*" Brahim said, nodding and shaking Dylan's hand, "*insha'Allah.*"

"*Y'allah,*" Faiz repeated, throwing the old van into gear and driving away with Brahim and Bouhouch running alongside the van, still holding Dylan's hands.

"*B'slama!*" Dylan said, releasing his grip and waving goodbye to his friends who stood waving in the dusty road.

Dylan stuck his head out the window as Faiz gained speed. The wind caught his old purple and grey cap, now frayed at the brim. Dylan reached for it as it blew, but knowing it was lost, he returned to wave once again to his friends. Brahim and Bouhouch stood in the dusty road waving—and now laughing—in the faint light of morning. *Mashi mushkil.*

By the time Maryam returned with the morning's water, Ibrahim had buried the infant in the cemetery, leaving no marker for the grave. Heleema and Aisha had left for school and Amina and Hassan warmed themselves in the courtyard sunlight. Fatoum and Saida tidied the house, speaking nothing of the baby. Life had resumed.

"Keep yourselves busy today, do not trouble your mother." Saida again admonished the children before setting out for the hills.

Maryam had less work with Fatoum healthy again, but the goats remained her chore.

"Mama, I will feed the goats now," she said, reaching to kiss Fatoum's hand.

"*Wa-ha*, Maryam, *ihallah*," Fatoum patted Maryam's back.

"You are early. Tafouit sits low in the sky," the billy said as she opened the gate.

"Today is different. Today we go to the west," Maryam said.

"Do not worry, we can return to the oasis. Taggat is gone," the billy consoled.

"I know," Maryam said, thinking not of Taggat but of the cemetery. "*Y'allah*, we will go this way," and she threw a stone at the herd to push them toward the west. The billy pushed the herd along, more pleasant and amiable than Taggat.

"Where is the grass?" he asked Maryam as they walked.

"Just there, where the *oued* once flowed."

Approaching the small embankment, they saw the green oasis with fresh water come into view, and they bleated happily. The animals contented themselves with the verdant grass and clear water while Maryam again looked to the mountains far away. *This is my life,* she thought. *The others will go over the mountains, but I will stay, insha'Allah.*

"You will care for your parents and your grandmother. It is good," the billy said, interrupting her thoughts as he ate. Maryam walked to the trickling stream and scooped fresh water to her mouth—it tasted sweeter than the tap water she hauled every day. The oasis she found made the goats strong, and the water she drew from the rocks made her work easier than for other women in the village. *It is good,* she thought. While the oasis was never free from danger—as the threat of Tifigrah always remained close in the desert—she and her goats found peace there, and for that, she gave thanks.

Igdi limped alongside Maryam as they returned to the village late that afternoon. His shadow stretched across the stony ground while she cast none.

"Afraid to return to the east?" he barked. Maryam threw a stone as her response. Igdi turned to limp, but she stopped him.

"How did you survive Tifigrah?"

"I was young and strong, but Taggat was old and the bite deep. That is the way of the desert, girl. Nothing remains of her, the desert took her back," he barked, turning away.

Maryam returned to the house to find her mother and grandmother drinking tea and eating almonds. The young girls busied themselves with a crude jump-rope while Hassan sat by the door, again playing with his thin plastic bag. Entering the salon, Maryam politely greeted them both and turned to the almost-empty water jugs.

"Come and sit, Maryam," said Fatoum while Saida poured a fresh glass of sugary mint tea for her granddaughter. "You work so hard, child."

"Yes, the water will last a while longer. Come and drink," the old woman said.

"*Shukran, Mahallu,*" Maryam said as she took the glass to sip.

In the distance, the faint voice of the *muezzin* fell like dew over the village and again called the faithful to sunset prayers, heralding the Saharan moon.

"*Ihallah, Mahallu,*" Maryam said to her grandmother. "That is the way of the desert."

Afterword

Writing About Wandering

Three themes exist at the heart of this triptych: landscape description, characterization, and magical realism. In the first story, the eponymous hero Dylan travels from the city of Marrakech across a wild landscape to his new home in the desert mountains of southern Morocco. Just as his enthusiasm for his assignment diminishes, the grandeur of the Atlases unfolds before him, thereby tying his anxiety to the fearsomeness of his new world in a way similar to Bowles. In "Bou Gafr," Dylan's emotions continue to vacillate between anxiety and confidence until he confronts the power of the wilderness like the Ait 'Atta tribesmen had seventy-five years earlier on the same mountain, reconciling some of the tension of his desert life. Resolution comes in the third story, "Maryam," where the reader—now familiar with the desert landscape—unexpectedly encounters the mystical through the eyes of a teenage Tamazight heroine, moving the reader from Dylan's outsider perspective to a more intimate understanding of the Sahara. This shift reflects Dylan's growth over two stories and two years as he moves almost, but not quite, from outsider to insider. My desert is a place of wander; it is a setting that kindles human emotion through the very experience of that place—much like the experience of Asouf in al-Koni's *The Bleeding of the Stone*. Like al-Koni and al-Tahawy, I bind my characters' growth to their mastery of the desert. My work differs insofar as Dylan—even with his change over time—remains a bit of an outsider in this new world, perhaps even more than Bowles' escapist Moresbys.

This desert landscape provides a context for Dylan's wander, and the journey story—known as *rihla*—serves as a central theme in Arabic literature. Across all three stories, Dylan experiences wander in different ways: as a geographic journey, as emotional healing, and as a gradual discovery of faith. Dylan wanders: first from Marrakech to Ikniouen in "Dylan," then to the summit of the fearsome mountain of Bou Gafr, and lastly, as he prepares to return to the United States in "Maryam." I try to match the symbolism of my desert descriptions to his various physical experiences in the wilderness. The arc of the story encompasses Dylan's emotional healing, which can be viewed as his second journey. He is tested in the desert when he encounters not only memories of his former fiancée, Kayla, but also people who stir up emotions with which he must reconcile in order to heal. Gradually, he finds a gentle faith in the wilderness, comprising the last example of Dylan's wander, thereby tying the work to more ancient examples of the Islamic *rihla* as well as the Christian desert experience.

Like the authors I mentioned in the Foreword, I try to create meaningful desert descriptions as a space for characters to *stravaig*. Some characters are, of course, developed more fully than others in the space of the short stories, but characterization has been a major component of this project. I have carefully tried to avoid Said's Orientalism by forming authentic descriptions of Moroccans in these stories, and I have spent much time developing three characters in particular: in the first two stories, the American hero Dylan, and in the last piece, the heroine

Maryam and her archetypal grandmother Saida.

Like Bowles's confident Port, Dylan is not ready for the desert, and yet, like Kit—and probably a little better than she—he emerges from the wilderness stronger and healed some two years later. At times, I think of Dylan as a typical white, middle-class American from Generation X. He shows himself to be bright, and even thoughtful, but decidedly average. Dylan is an Everyman for his time. Perhaps like Luke Skywalker, or maybe even most heroes, Dylan emerges from ordinary beginnings, embarks on a journey while burdened, and finds enlightenment. Dylan is not the flashy hero of fantasy, but a real one for the twenty-first century. He exits the stories as the person he should have been at the start, which is quite different from the broken character of Kit at the end of *The Sheltering Sky*. Like the character Maryam, Dylan is entirely a creation; the circumstances of my Peace Corps service were different from his. Bouhouch, Brahim, and Faiz are the names of friends I made during my service in the mountain village of Ikniouen, but the stories told here are fiction.

Crafting Maryam presented the biggest challenge for me as a writer because I wanted to avoid both stereotype and a Cinderella character who evolves through the proverbial rags-to-riches journey. Maryam is poor and misunderstood like Cinderella, but discovers contentment—not happiness—in her mountain life rather than with a prince in a castle. I struggled to find the voice of an impoverished, adolescent Tamazight teenage girl, and yet, her simple vocabulary and limited world-view are, I think, representative of her basic schooling. I also noticed these elements in al-Tahawy's Fatima. North African folklore shapes Maryam's worldview just like Fatima and other Tamazight women. Even with her embrace of tradition, Maryam is a woman of the twenty-first century. She does not stand outside of time, and she, her family, Dylan, and the reader all question her place in the contemporary world. Maryam's name draws on the Christian and Qur'anic respect for Mary, who also seems to have faced misunderstandings as a girl.

Less developed is the archetypal character of Maryam's grandmother, Saida. Professor William Granara first introduced the grandmother archetype to me in his Modern Arabic Fiction course at Harvard University. I include Saida to both situate my writing within the broader context of the genre, as well as to offer a "villainous" counterpoint to Maryam's purity. Saida represents an amalgamation of many similar village grandmothers in the twenty-first century who devotedly scrounge for fuel every day to keep their families warm during the night.

I balance the realistic narrative of Dylan's journey with the mysticism of the desert as shown by al-Koni and al-Tahawy. Despite a wasteland and an apparent place of death, the Sahara is a tantalizing place of oases—a truth I want to capture, but not through Dylan's foreign eyes. As an outsider, he never fully penetrates the desert's mysteries like Maryam. Here, I again drew inspiration from native authors like al-Koni and al-Tahawy. Maryam senses—she sees, hears, and feels—things that the others of the tribe cannot. Her interior experiences set Maryam apart from the rest of the village, while Dylan—always an outsider—plays the part of an ordinary character. Impoverished, broken, and holding a single woman's role in a patriarchal world, Maryam has a fuller, more enriching experience of the desert village than the other girls or even Dylan. When Dylan looks at her, he sees the obvious limitations of her socio-economic position, and yet, through the story, the reader discovers the beauty of her life. The presence of talking animals in the story, like Taggat and Igdi, evoke North African folktales like those of the Jackal and the Hedgehog, which I found printed in a 1901 tome: *Moorish Literature Comprising Romantic Ballads, Tales of the Berbers, Stories of the Kabylie, Folklore, and National Traditions.* I derived animal names from the regional Tashelheet dialect, with "Taggat" meaning she-goat and "Igdi" meaning a male dog. While I spend more of the first two stories crafting a realistic Saharan landscape, "Maryam" represents an attempt to include the richness and timelessness of desert mythology into my contemporary composition. With acknowledgment to Bowles, my stories grapple with the hubris of the young American's journey while at the same time shaping a symbolic setting for the traditional Arabic journey-story, or *rihla*, in the Sahara.

Glossary of Moroccan Words

The following Arabic and Tashelheet phrases are used in the stories:

afak: please

Amazigh: "the free people," the indigenous North Africans

andu: we go

asmuninu: my friend

b'slama: goodbye

Berber: indigenous North Africans, from the Greek

bezzef: a lot, much

bismillah: in the name of God

bla jmil: you're welcome

chal: how much?

djellaba: long, loose-fitting outer garment from North Africa

douar: a desert village encircling an open space

hajj: an elder who presumably made the pilgrimage to Mecca

hanoot: store, shop

hijab: a woman's headscarf that exposes the face

ihallah: good

insha'Allah: God willing

ishka: difficult

izran: rocks

kulshi: everything

l'hamdullah/l'hamdulillah: Thanks be to God

labas: well

l-fsa: desert scrub brush

m'bruk: congratulations

mah: why

mahallu: grandmother

mani: where

mashi mushkil: no problem

meskeen: poor

metsharfin: nice to meet you

mezyan: very good

muezzin: man who calls Muslims to prayer from a minaret

mumtaz: well done, good job

nhas: copper (bullets)

nukta: joke

oued: riverbed

safi: enough

salamu alaykum: peace be upon you

samhi: forgive me, sorry

shukran: thank you

shwiya: a little, not good

souq: market (bazaar)

su: drink (imperative verb)

tagine: a Moroccan cooking pot and its contents

Tamazight: feminine for *Amazigh*

Tashelheet: Amazigh dialect

tish: eat (imperative verb)

ur sinugh: I do not know

usted: teacher

waaa: exclamation, like "hey!"

wa-ha: ok

y'allah: let's go

For Further Reading

al-Koni, Ibrahim. *The Bleeding of the Stone*. Translated by May Jayyusi and Christopher Tingley, Interlink Publishing, 2002.

al-Tahawy, Miral. *The Tent*. Translated by Anthony Calderbank, American Univ. in Cairo Press, 1996.

Bowles, Paul. *The Sheltering Sky*. The Library of America, 2002.

Calleja, Meinrad. *The Philosophy of Desert Metaphors in Ibrahim al-Koni*. FARAXA, 2012.

Cather, Willa. *Death Comes for the Archbishop*. Vintage, 1990.

Dib, Mohammed. *The Savage Night*. Translated by C. Dickson, Univ. of Nebraska Press, 1995.

Hart, David. *Dadda 'Atta and his Forty Grandsons: The Socio-Political Organization of the Ait 'Atta of Southern Morocco*. MENAS Press Limited, 1981.

Idris, Yusuf. *The Sinners*. Translated by Kristin Peterson-Ishaq, Lynne Rienner Publishers, 2009.

Le Clézio, J.M.G. *Desert.* Translated by C. Dickson, David R. Godine Publishers, 2009.

Lévi-Strauss, Claude. *Triste Tropiques.* Translated by John Weightman. Jonathan Cape, 1973.

Mahfouz, Naguib. *Midaq Alley.* Translated by Trevor Le Gassiek, Anchor Books, 1966.

—-. *The Journey of Ibn Fattouma.* Translated by Denys Johnson-Davies, Anchor Books, 1993.

Moorish Literature Comprising Romantic Ballads, Tales of the Berbers, Stories of the Kabylie, Folklore, and National Traditions. Translated by Rene Basset and Chauncey C. Starkweather, The Colonial Press, 1901.

Ondaatje, Michael. *The English Patient.* McClelland & Stewart, Inc., 1992.

Rifaat, Alifa. *Distant View of a Minaret.* Heinemann, 1988.

Said, Edward. *Orientalism.* Vintage Books, 1979.

Acknowledgement

I am grateful to my parents, Paul and Debbie, for teaching me, among other things, how to hold a pencil. At Oakmont Regional High School, I had the good fortune to learn from the late Elma Cancellieri as well as Diane Erickson who continues to read my writing today. Professors Susan Gabriel, Fr. Benedict Guevin, O.S.B., and Sean Goodlett refined my post-secondary composition, while Joan Hunter also helped cultivate my skills. I am indebted to the scholars who shaped my Harvard studies, most notably William Granara, Ken Urban, Christina Thompson, and especially Karen Heath who generously read my work and helped me ask more meaningful questions. Since 2011, the Oakmont community has become my family, including David Uminski, Dana Altobelli, Audrey Phelps, Tim Caouette, and David Lantry, while former Oakmonter Carolyn Tobia expertly proofread this work. Like Virgil, Kris DeMoura guides my creativity and it is my great privilege to direct theatre with him. I thank my favorite student, my sister Jenn, for modeling kindness during our four Oakmont years. *Shukran*.

About the Author

Jeffrey William Aubuchon returned to Oakmont Regional High School in 2011, after a thirteen-year absence in which he traveled the world and volunteered with the Peace Corps. Beyond directing theatre and teaching history, he advises the student group apush4peace that continues to raise thousands of dollars for Peace Corps projects worldwide. When not enjoying the forests of Massachusetts, he wanders among the Joshua trees of California's Mojave Desert. He studied in the liberal arts tradition with the Benedictine monks and faculty of Saint Anselm College, where he graduated *magna cum laude*, and later earned a master's degree from the creative writing faculty at Harvard University.

Photo by Sue O'Connor of www.sueoconnorphotography.com.

You can connect with me on:
- http://jeffreywaubuchon.com
- https://twitter.com/JeffreyAubuchon

Also by Jeffrey W. Aubuchon

Flight School: Lessons with Peter Pan

The students of Oakmont Regional High School in Massachusetts looked to soar just like Mary Martin when they staged *Peter Pan* in 2018 as their annual musical. Over the span of eighteen months, the cast—along with their classmates, teachers, parents, and rural community—learned to fly in the most unexpected of ways. *Flight School* tells the dramatic journey of this community brought together by a century-old story and the financial, technical, and social challenges these students overcame in their theatrical voyage to Neverland. You'll believe you can fly, too! Available from 92252 Press in June 2020.

www.ingramcontent.com/pod-product-compliance
Lightning Source LLC
Chambersburg PA
CBHW050151110726
47898CB00008B/2753